LANCE AND QUILL

CHRONICLE ENTRY 9

Azalea Dabill

Dynamos Press

Coeur d' Alene, Idaho

Dynamos Press
Coeur d' Alene, Idaho/83815
www.azaleadabill.com

Publisher's Note: This is a work of fiction. Names, characters, places, and incidents are a product of the author's imagination. Locales and public names are sometimes used for atmospheric purposes. Any resemblance to actual people, living or dead, or to businesses, companies, events, institutions, or locales is completely coincidental.

All Scripture quotes from NASB except for a few words substituted for meaning. "Scripture quotations taken from the New American Standard Bible®, Copyright © 1960, 1962, 1963, 1968, 1971, 1972, 1973,1975, 1977, 1995 by The Lockman Foundation Used by permission." (www.Lockman.org)

Book Layout ©2015 BookDesignTemplates.com

Cover Design photos from Fotolia

Cover Design by Derek Murphy

Quantity sales. Special discounts are available on quantity purchases by corporations, associations, and others. For details, contact the "Special Sales Department" at the address above.

Keywords: medieval romance, epic fantasy series, martial arts fiction, Christian adventure, young adult and teens epic fantasy book series, historical fantasy fiction

Lance and Quill Entry 9/ Azalea Dabill. -- 1st ed.
ISBN 978-1-943034-02-4

Contents

Lance and Quill

To Gloria B.,
Encourager extraordinaire, an adventurer in her own way, and with
gratitude to the many others who follow in her steps.

THE FALCON CHRONICLES

FALCON HEART CHRONICLE I

FALCON FLIGHT CHRONICLE II

FALCON DAGGER CHRONICLE III *

LANCE AND QULL - A NOVELLA

FALCON'S ODE - POETRY COMPANION

Suggested Reading Order

Two prequels in *Falcon Dagger* *Coming 2024

Falcon Heart a novel

Falcon Flight a novel

Lance and Quill a novella

Falcon Dagger three novellas.

Of Chronicle Books and Entries

If you are reading *Lance and Quill* as a stand-alone book, skip this introduction. Spoiler's ahead. If you've read any of the *Chronicle* or *Chronicle Entries* and want to know where this companion *Entry* picks up—read on!

In *Chronicle I: Falcon Heart,* Kyrin Cieri of Cierheld finds adventure beyond fear.

Slavers seize Kyrin from the coast of medieval Britannia and sail for Araby. With a dagger from her murdered mother's hand, an exiled warrior from the East, and a peasant girl, Kyrin finds mystery, martial skill, and friendship closer than blood.

The falcon dagger pursues her through tiger-haunted dreams, love, and war in the Araby sands. Caught by the caliph's court intrigue, stronghold daughter Kyrin Cieri faces the blade that killed her mother, and overcomes treachery in Oman.

The sequel, *Falcon Flight: Chronicle II,* begins two years later in Ali Ben Aidon's house in Oman.

Dying, Kyrin's master Ali Ben Aidon holds a grudge against the three companions, while Kyrin yearns to return to her father in Britannia. Guest for a night, Sirius Abdasir, wazir to the caliph, sets the companions on a new road. He executes Ali for treachery, holds Tae for his knowledge of the death touch, and sends Kyrin and Alaina to Britannia to find a lost traveler as the price of their freedom.

Kyrin defies him, looses Tae, and leaves Tae and Alaina in Araby while she goes on the wazir's errand to Britannia alone.

There she fights for her life, her people, and her land against ambitious men, godless monks, and a hidden hand of treachery. An armsman's loyalty, a new stepmother, an unknown brother, and her father's love challenge her search for the wazir's traveler. From Arabia to Britannia, from slave to warrior, from fearful stronghold daughter to keeper of the keys, Kyrin Cieri unwittingly guards the secret of her murdered mother's falcon dagger. Troubled love, a jealous rival, the haunting tiger, and the falcon dagger hold doom—doom for Kyrin, her stronghold, and her companions. Or the keys of hope.

Lance and Quill: Chronicle Entry 9, relates Alaina's adventures when she leaves Kyrin to her quest and flees with Tae into the sands—to Faisal, desert prince of the Twilkets. Forsaking rose perfume and Ali's court gardens, Alaina escapes the wazir's Hand.

But the wazir's reach is long. A slave who runs must be caught—and the wazir sends an army against Faisal's tents, where a traitor lurks in the Oasis of Oaths.

So begins a war for freedom, justice, love . . .

This is Alaina's story.

In apology to any who feel cheated that I wrote this companion book before the sequel, *Falcon Flight: Chronicle II*—I wrote this for a dear friend who was excited about what happened to Faisal and Kyrin's romance in *Chronicle I* and who might not be here to read *Falcon Flight*, though I hope she may see many more books than this. With all my love . . .

1

Hearts of Change

But the Lord looks at the heart. ~ 1 Samuel 16:7

Alaina stared into the darkness beyond the glowing coals. Sand whispered, sliding up the dunes with the wind. Doubtless Faisal did not know he treated her as Nara's kitchen help when he gave her his dish to scour with sand. Around the night fire, she broke her silence. "You were kind to take my message to Seliam."

Faisal rested his arms on his knees, his strong hands quiet. "He did not tell the *wazir* of my presence, which was all I asked. Do not judge Seliam too harshly. Captain to Sirius Abdasir, the wazir of the caliph, he is torn between debt of blood and debt of word—between your sister who held his life and his master who holds his oath—and now you, who hold his friendship."

"I? Hold his friendship? I think not." *Traitor.*

"The prince's words are true." Kentar nodded agreement. Veteran camel driver that he was, his *thawb* was drawn close against the desert chill. His old gaze was sharp, the wrinkles of his dark face driven deep by many caravan journeys.

Eyes prickling, Alaina bit her lip. The prince lived up to his name. Faisal Ben Salin, the just judge. Where thanks was due, she would give it. Yet she would *not* quickly absolve Seliam, once a friend. He deserted them when his master held those she loved captive to his dangerous will. It did not matter whether Sirius Abdasir was the caliph's wazir, or the caliph himself. A friend did not leave friends in danger.

The firelight blurred. Alaina pulled her knees up, laid her head down, and stirred the edge of the fire into flame. A Twilket prince must not see her tears. She *could* be as fierce as Kyrin.

Soon Tae banked the fire and they bedded down. The exiled healer and warrior was dear to her as a second father, but he could not comfort her heart this time. She was too weary for more words, but in the bottom of the dune-bowl, sleep left her. She could almost hear Kyrin stir restlessly, see her long shadow beyond the eyes of the coals. But her sister closer than blood did not sleep there, and might never return.

Alaina bit the back of her hand against tears. Kyrin had given her word to Sirius Abdasir that she would fulfill his task, but it was not enough. The wazir had taken Tae as their bond. Alaina's lip curled.

She and Kyrin did not trust Sirius to keep Tae from harm in the roiling currents of the caliph's court in these days of heavy taxes, uneasy slaves, and whispers of rebellion in Baghdad. They snatched Tae from his hands and rode into the desert. After that defiance, Kyrin refused to let her and Tae within Sirius's reach. Her sister had boarded the wazir's ship on the Red Sea at Jedda alone, bound for Britannia on the wazir's errand.

Now Kyrin searched the hills and forests of Britannia for a life in exchange for theirs. When she found Hamal, the one lost to the wazir, would the wazir lose interest in their heads? Doubtless he fixed their price, when he knew she and Tae fled back to the sands.

For every act there was a price. Alaina squeezed her eyes shut, and her mouth twisted in pain. Why had Tae shown Kyrin the touch of death and not her? They had always trained in the way of the warrior together. From the beginning.

She heard his voice again in the night silence of the dunes. A stray breeze had brought his words from behind a mountain of sand where he took Kyrin aside. "The touch of death is for none other than your hands. Do you hear me, my daughter? . . . You go into peril. The death touch is for greatest need . . ." The rest of Tae's words had been swept away.

Alaina shivered and curled into a ball. She might also need the death touch. Umar led his Hand of salukis and the wazir's men after them, seeking that very knowledge. And when he learned it—but the wazir must catch them first.

The night chill carved icy holes for the stars, and her breath plumed. She could feel Tae behind her, a hunched blot sitting against the sand ridge, his back to Kentar, who was his eyes and ears among the desert tribes.

Alaina rolled over. Near the top of the sand-bowl, Faisal kept watch with his stallion. Zahir was a beast clean of limb, with the small Araby head and proud carriage, a veritable dark wind of the desert. Like his master, he belonged to this harsh land.

She sniffed, not altogether disdainfully. Faisal must keep the peace in the Oasis of Oaths, which stood as witness between Aneza and Twilket, with a swift lance, swifter horses, and a heart as wild as the dark wolf that haunted the mountains in the cool shadows before the dawn. Doubtless when he lifted his lance many Twilket warriors answered his call.

He and Kyrin walked after the same Lord now, rode the same wind. Once they had not. But her sister was gone from his reach, bound to seek Hamal. She returned to her father, a lord in Britannia in his own right, for Kyrin was heir to Cierheld stronghold.

Alaina looked at her hands. They smelled of gritty earth. She was only a peasant, though a sister to Kyrin, closer than blood.

She closed her eyes. A tear tickled around her ear, headed for the sand below. Her family was gone, killed the day she was enslaved, fallen alongside the baker's boy she might have hand-fasted. All gone.

Now all was taken again. She had been so near to being a scribe to the caliph, the highest ruler in this land. Her delicate, dedicated hand in his court would have won her freedom. Her hand was skilled at many things. The softest silk and cotton thawbs, rose and jasmine scents for her skin and hair would have been hers, with embroidery thread of all hues for every garment she could imagine and put her needle to, which would have gained her the favor of the women of the court.

She had been so near, so close to a name as a scribe, even a poet of verse. A creator of word and writ who drew all who heard her into a place of vivid thought and sharpened spirit. Alaina choked on a bitter sob. Now she would be surprised to see *Alaina Ilen* gracing the odd scrap of untanned hide she might rescue from some tentmaker and pen a few words on. She drew a breath and wiped her face. Enough.

Desert Bedouin had little use for writing, and less for a female scribe. She was done with rosewater. But Faisal's ailing *sheyk* would need her knowledge of herbs, though many others had that skill. Tae had taught her well in it.

The sand behind her hip was rough and cold and hard. Her exile was just begun. Were only herbs and her needle to be left to her?

If she could but see Kyrin again and hear the bards raise their clear, thunderous voices around the fires under the oaks of Britannia. Better now if she had gone to scribe for her sister.

For if Umar's Hand caught them, or a warrior betrayed them for coin before Kyrin found Hamal . . . Alaina swallowed.

Did Cicero hunt or did his paws carry him far over the sand, his loyal hound's heart yearning for Kyrin? His comforting nose was elsewhere, his moon-shadow form blending with the night. Would Umar's Hand tear him to shreds also?

Chilled, Alaina turned over. Dawn was coming in a few bells. Did Kyrin see the same stars spangled across the sky—did a dark and dangerous expanse lean over her?

§

"Tae!" Alaina bolted upright in her blanket, grasping for her staff, and rolled to her feet. She held the weapon across her chest, blinking. Her nose stung with frost.

Sharp barks echoed, high and far. Cold first light bared dark hills beyond a far line of dunes. The dry and pungent smell of seared herbage and sand was unbroken.

The men around her waited, silent and still, listening. Tae held the noses of the two nearest horses, and Faisal restrained his stallion and her mare. The Twilket prince lifted his head in the old gesture. His nostrils flared as a wolf's, his eyes dark in his lean face. He held a ready lance; his other hand rested an unusual camel stick across his beast's withers. Alaina gulped, trying to steady her breathing.

Nothing escaped Tae, exiled *hwarang* warrior from the East— even if the caliph and his wazir did hunt them across the Araby sands. Tae would have awoken her earlier if danger were close.

He nudged dry camel dung into the ashy remains of the night fire at his feet. A clear tongue of flame rose. He glanced at her over the smokeless blaze. "Cicero hunts." The wrinkles of a silent laugh deepened about his almond eyes. No man who saw the white hair about his ear from an old wound, stark against the straight-cropped black, and met his steady gaze would make the mistake that lack of height made him prey. Alaina licked her lips. It was only Cicero who had awoken her.

She kept her gaze from Faisal. A prince of the Twilkets must not see her night-fears. The saluki barked again, fainter. Beside Tae, young Youbib of the Aneza grinned, a flash of teeth against dark skin under his turban, and Alaina's tight grip on her staff relaxed.

Kentar nodded, his wrinkled face creasing within the frame of his white *kaffiyeh,* and muttered to Youbib, "It is not the Hand. Umar and his pack do not come for us."

Alaina clamped her jaw on the laugh she could not stop if she once let it go, and bent to roll up her bed. Her eyes were as gritty as if they had slept bare moments. Her heart yet thundered.

Umar's Hand would not be merciful. She shivered. Brought down by saluki teeth and claws, then beaten with sticks, sewn in a raw hide—wounded, left in the sun to the delight of ants, wasps, and dung beetles—unable to move while they crawled and bit and gnawed . . . the wazir's swift blade through the neck might be a gift. She would give Cicero a bit of her meat at the night fire for not being Umar's Hand—his pack of salukis and the wazir's men—who hunted them. She shifted her rolled blanket under her arm and lifted her eyes to the sky. Where was Truthseeker? They must leave.

§

Faisal lifted his head and gave a piercing whistle. Kentar jerked his blade a fraction from his sheath in reflex—then slid it home with a pointed glare. Faisal shrugged, grinned, and lifted his arm toward the brightening blue sky. There was an answering scream.

Truthseeker thumped onto his wrist, driving his arm toward earth. He kept her up with an effort, biting back a grimace. He had not been able to teach her to land as if alighting at her eyrie. His arm was no rabbit.

Truthseeker cocked her head and uttered a softer cry. Faisal stroked the falcon's head and down her back. She arched her neck, straightening with a ruffle of feathers and a proud wag of her tail. "Ahh my wise one, tell me, does Cicero chase a rabbit or a *reem?*"

She shifted taloned feet toward his shoulder and bobbed her head, her piercing amber gaze on Alaina. Alaina stared back, wide-eyed as the reem, the gazelle. She clutched her blanket, her knuckles white. Faisal's brow wrinkled as he tilted his head toward the falcon.

"It is only Kyrin's Truthseeker. She is a queen among the noble ones, swift and deadly. Since the peace, she has come into her own, a true shaheen. Here"—he held out the peregrine— "you hunt with her this day."

Alaina stepped back, pulling her blanket close, biting her lip. Red-gold hair peeped from her rumpled kaffiyeh, slipping to one side. She had been Tae's wife in name, along with Kyrin, though Tae treated them as daughters, despite their master's command. Then the wazir had executed Ali for treason, and they were free of him. Faisal knew Tae had honored the Master of the Stars in the matter of marriage and watched for an opportunity to return to his treasured wife, Huen, in the Land of the Morning Calm.

Faisal shrugged. "As you will it." There was enough fear in the world. He would not add to it. A peregrine could tear a man's eyes from him as he ran.

Alaina might well be cautious of Truthseeker. One did need a strong arm, and the falcon's talons were sharp. She would rest on Zahir's saddle while they ate and broke camp. He sighed. He knew fear—beyond the Hand that trailed them.

Truthseeker spread her wings again and settled. Her soft cream breast was dotted with black, her feathers gleamed steel blue and grey, barred with black. The teardrop markings about her eyes made her a wise queen, one who knew the hearts of men. She had no conspiracy of tongues or hidden blades about her. Faisal's lips crept back from his teeth as he stroked her. The falcon did not hunt any creature's blood except to eat.

Would that she could instruct his grandfather's first warrior, Hafiz. Could reveal to him that his prince thirsted for the freedom of sand and rock and wind, the peace of mountain shade at midday, the laughter of children about their games, and the voices of women gathered about the night fires with jars of water from the spring of the Oasis of Oaths. That Faisal Ben Salin, prince of the Twilkets, thirsted for nothing greater than the pounding blood of the hunt, to race after black-horned reem beside his Twilket brothers, to hone the edge of watchfulness needed to guard caravans on their perilous way across the sands.

Faisal's mouth tightened. Far better to face swords and lances than tongues drawn behind tent curtains and words cast at his back. Weapons could be turned aside. The Araby sands did not taunt him as Hafiz's tongue so often did.

Which of them would be sheyk when his grandfather passed? That was the question that pricked his heart. He would that he *could* give his place to Hafiz—that was the sorrow of it.

The oath of the Light of Blood, or the Nur-ed-Dam, the blood fued between Aneza and Twilket, was ended, paid for by the ceded Oasis of Oaths. Tae brought about the end of that war. Youbib of the Aneza rode with them as surety of it.

Faisal smiled crookedly. Thus, Hafiz's ongoing oath of blood against Tae and Alaina and Kyrin was twice unlawful. Hafiz yearned for many things.

Alaina looked away from his stare, her blanket under her arm. Faisal blinked. He yearned for peace, for time in which to build up his people, but she must think his wits thick as honey. Face heating, he handed the mare's rein to her, and she led the beast aside. Fastening her blanket behind its saddle, she murmured in its twitching ear, her voice clear and beautiful.

Faisal nudged Truthseeker off his arm and onto Zahir's pommel. The stallion sighed and stamped a dark hoof as the prince slid his lance into its carrying thongs and stroked the horse's warm neck. Faisal raised his face to the sky and the heat creeping over the rim of the world. The sands held sun and shadow, gaunt death and stark beauty. In the desert of his birth one had water or one did not.

He met Tae's brown gaze. "It will be good for my Twilket brothers to see you, a warrior at my back. It will be good for them to know sheyk Gershem Ben Salin of the Twilkets may yet live. If you cure the weariness sucking the life from my grandfather—our people might outlast Hafiz, the wazir, and the caliph's taxes together."

Tae nodded, strong and sure.

But more was needed than lance and wit against their enemies. Faisal touched the haft of his dagger. His brothers needed him to lead them through the path of blood ahead.

The open spaces called to him—the quiet and the far hunt, but blood could not be avoided—and his own rose in answer. If the desert was to have peace and not be overrun by caliph officials demanding coin, camels, and more precious things, they must fight. If it took blood to keep men such as Tae and his brothers from the caliph and the wazir's Hand, so be it.

Truthseeker preened. Faisal reached inside his saddlebag for a small hood and bell. Deftly, he covered her head and sharp beak and looped the bell about her foot. It tinkled. Cicero would come soon, following Alaina's scent as they rode. His nose was uncommonly keen. As keen as the wazir's Hand.

Alaina glanced at him, and Faisal stared back, grim. It was time to eat and ride. They would need their strength. He nodded to Kentar, who dug into the packs on Tae's beast. Kentar stirred something into the pot Tae had rigged over the crackling fire, as Tae dropped in a dusting of dark powder.

Faisal hoped it was not more of the fiery red pepper and soured vegetables. Boiled meat or dried dates would be a feast, but what Tae called "kimchi" would burn a hole in any man's belly. He grimaced. Though he supposed what it did not burn, it strengthened for their flight.

Tae studied his creation in the pot as impassively as he did his enemies, the satisfied lines around his mouth belying his round face. There was more to his wise, implacable will than kimchi. His hair held a heavier peppering of white over the black of two seasons ago, when he held sheyk Gershem of the Twilkets under his blade and lived to speak of it.

Faisal dug his fingers into the warm bowl of food Tae handed him and sniffed. Rice and dates, with a hint of cinnamon.

"Is it good, desert prince?" Tae laughed at him.

Faisal shrugged and took a pointed taste. And smiled. He ate swiftly.

Alaina bit her lip and looked away. Did she laugh also? Clad in the manner of the desert in his brothers' robe-like thawb and flowing kaffiyeh to hide her bright hair and womanly form, she joined Tae and the others on the far side of the fire, dipping into her bowl hastily with slender fingers. Her garb was as stiff as his with the sweat of five sunrises of riding.

She rubbed her dirty face, looking as weary as he. Cicero had taken a reward from her hand at the fire delicately, his head and jaws silver-grey, the rest of his form touched with shadow.

His ears and whipcord body quivered as he gulped the meat and lifted his almond gaze to her face. His tail waved to and fro and he gave a short whine and touched his nose to her fingers. Then in a few long-legged bounds he was gone. If only they could escape so easily. The warm bowl threatened to break in Faisal's tightening fingers.

Umar had picked up their trail on the far side of the mountains, and now Tae's gaze never seemed to rest. He watched the hills and the mountains that rose in a vague chain behind them on their left, and turned often toward the great sands that spread eastward in dunes higher than any wind-tower. The way ahead was long and rocky. Kentar watched their trail behind, a long range of granite peaks disappearing toward the south. The cinnamon soured in Faisal's nose. He, a wolf of the desert, fled before a hyena.

Tae cleaned the cooking things and put them on his horse. Alaina crouched beside his empty place, cleaning her bowl. She lifted her heart-shaped face, and her green gaze caught on Faisal, as startled as a rabbit gone down to drink, frozen beside a wadi pool. Her lashes fluttered down, and her cheeks colored. Her hair held the same flame.

Faisal swallowed his last date, dipped his bowl full of sand, scoured it, and dumped it into the fire. It snuffed out. He was fallen in Alaina's esteem for her sister's sake, over their old quarrel. Apprenticed in the way of the warrior and the healer, Alaina doubtless knew poisons. She was not one he wished to give more reason to fear or dislike him—more reason than a scorned sister. He kicked sand into the fire pit with sudden force.

Caliphs, wazirs, and Umar's Hand, they were full of vaporous dreams of power from breathing incense and eating too much rich meat. They made trouble for all who saw the majesty of the desert, who wished to trade and live in it by their wits, as men.

He sighed, and eyed Alaina sidelong. If Kyrin were here he would see a blaze kindle in her dark eyes, see her mouth firm into a line, her small-boned, strong form rise up across the fire pit, as determined as he. But she was not here. His mouth softened.

Did Alaina regret leaving Ali's gardens, the bathing pool of the women's courts, the flowers and fruit, the comforts of rosewater? She had gained sand and heat in their place—riding sores—the talk and sweat and food of men. She fled from swift danger into an uncertain future. Sandy spots dashed across her nose, slightly burned and peeling, for all it was near winter.

Faisal smiled faintly. The sun was ever fierce. As fierce as she. He'd seen her wield the staff now tied to her horse, the heavy wood as light as grass in her hands, *sissing* through the air.

Alaina blinked and turned away. A tear ran down and trembled on the end of her nose, ready to fall.

He suddenly wished he could take her for a fast gallop on Zahir. He would show her the beauty of the reem running over the sands, the dunes flowering in glory after a rain, and wipe away that tear. He would make her smile. Might the skin around her green eyes crinkle, might her mouth resemble the gentle curve of a moon across water? She had lost many things. She would not lose her life to Umar's Hand of salukis.

He would do what he could. Faisal stood and held out his bowl. She might come to name him something other than jackal. When one could not escape an unpleasant thought, the best thing was a task to lose oneself in.

Alaina dragged her arm across her eyes, shot him a glare that could burn wood to cinder, reached to grab the bowl out of his hand, and stalked toward the pack camel. He stared after her with a frown. Prickly she was, but they must ride. Would they see the sun to its rest? He did not know. But they would show Umar and his Hand how the hunted could run.

2

The Hand

You have made my heart beat faster with a single glance. ~ Song of S 4:9

Umar lifted his head. They had gone, disappeared into the vastness of sand and stone. A cloudburst had spattered the earth, wiping out tracks and scent in a wash of running rivulets. On either side and behind him the sand lay unchanged. Ahead, the swath of green springing up after the rain stretched out of sight into the mountainous dunes.

The three men of the tents behind him had given him welcome for the night as desert law required. His salukis he left in the sands with his men and their tents. It was better his hosts thought him alone.

The elder spoke with his two sons in their cursed northern tongue, their heads together. They turned to him. The old one opened his mouth, several teeth missing.

"Servant of the most blessed, it is said the prince of the Twilkets is a very wolf of the sands." He gestured widely. "He is here, and there, and then gone. If Allah wills it, he may pasture his animals afar, since the rain makes the camel thorn and grass fat."

Umar said nothing. Patience brought fruit. If the old man's servant—who had left before the light with a few goats—went to warn the Twilket prince, he would know. He looked about him, sniffing the green smell. The wazir's enemies would not escape. None evaded his Hand.

The Kathirib tribe would enjoy these tents and animals. And he would rise to his rightful place as first guard to his master, the wazir, who rested in his new house in the Oman mountains. The rain-brightened sands brought the scent of sweet flowers.

Umar's breath came hard a moment. Ali Ben Aidon had never named him of his blood. In the end it was well he had not, for he did not meet the sword beside his father.

Umar's grip whitened on his dagger hilt. If Tae Chisun had trod light as a gazelle among the city merchants and desert tribesmen and had not spoken in the wrong ears of unjust taxes, Ali might yet rule his house. Yet Allah decreed otherwise.

A thin, mirthless smile tugged Umar's wide lips. Tae and his daughters who followed him were unbelieving *Nasrany.* One had gone. The other two would not outwit Allah's hand again. Umar snorted.

He would bring them to the wazir and extract their secret for his master's use. None knew if Tae had given his daughters knowledge of the touch of death. It might be kinder if he had not. Umar's mouth twisted, and he rubbed the scar across his hand.

Afterwards, Sirius would see his fitness for the place of over-seer and reward him. Who knew his old master's household as well as he, who knew which to bind, to bend them all to his master's will?

But there was one who did not bend. Jachin followed Tae even now, though it had brought him to chains. Chains. Tae Chisun might not let him extract the death touch without breaking him. If Tae willed it so, it would be done. For the most honorable, the most blessed of Allah. And Alaina, who loved the voice of Araby poets, would not hear them recite to a timbrel again. He had often tossed her staff to her when she fought before Ali's guests with her sister—the one who scarred him. Umar straightened his hand until a thin ridge of red-white flesh tightened to pain between his thumb and fingers.

Treacherous Nasrany, both of them. After her sister, Alaina had wormed her way into the household with the grace of a dancer and words of deceit, claiming to love all. They had chosen their path, set themselves to thwart him. And he had not seen it. For he let pass the matter of his hand when Kyrin helped Shema. He smiled bitterly. Shema—worthy to rule all Araby—though she lived in Ali's house. Her beauty was that of a gazelle's fawn, dark and lustrous. She might have lived to see him with favor . . . but that was past, and she was gone. Umar licked blood from his bitten lip.

He had chained Jachin in the courtyard to show his exalted new master the strength of his protection. Then Sirius Abdasir ordered Tae bound to keep the Nasrany women to their oath on his errand. Umar rubbed his forehead, looking over his shoulder at the desert tribesmen, who watched him. He set his jaw.

None of them understood. Even his mother did not. Alaina had poisoned the breast that nursed him. For Nara spat in his face when he held Jachin's chain in the courtyard that day. Then she ran within her kitchen and refused to see his face if he did not loose Jachin. Jachin, whose heart had ever followed Tae.

At last the Nasrany ran like dogs into the sands. Kyrin had sailed deceitfully on his master's ship. Where, he did not know. But she left two within his reach. Treacherous, all of them.

Umar turned to his host. The old man stepped back.

Umar smiled, satisfied. Opportunity had never looked on him—until Allah set his fate in his hands and bade him choose. That morning in the courtyard with Ali's severed head, he chose faithfulness. He released to their fate those who followed the path of faithlessness and the way of Djinn. He had no father. Now his master's enemies were his. Umar's mouth thinned.

Out in the sands a saluki raised its savage voice, and others of his Hand joined the chorus. They were strong, not as their weak brethren among the ignorant tribesmen. They desired blood, above loyalty. Well schooled, they were deadly beautiful as they streamed over a dune and into shadow.

Something akin rose in Umar. "As Allah wills it."

3

Staff and Quill

My tongue is the pen of a ready writer. ~ Psalms 45:1

Faisal's tents, a sun's journey beyond the Oasis of Oaths, where the mountains turned drier and smaller, was everything Alaina had hoped his camp would not be. The black tents of his people were too far from the Oasis where the Aneza stayed to ride and see Mey's friendly face, and it was certainly too far for a meal and a return before the setting sun. She would have liked to walk through the Oasis of Oaths again, to dabble her toes in the wadi spring that fed it, maybe swim in the clear pool. She wanted to feel again the moments of freedom when she was with Kyrin—and together they had been strong against those who opposed them.

Alaina shook her head, smiling faintly. She must record it before her memory grew dim. But no. She spent every moment in a stifling tent, watching old blade-tongued Gershem regain his strength.

"Boy!"

She bit the inside of her lip. She did not even have a moment to read the Master of the Star's Book before the sun rose. Mouth tightening, she turned.

The sheyk's wrinkled neck reminded her of a proud, naked buzzard's, his obsidian eyes bright. Against the weariness and lack of appetite that had shriveled him to pale skin and bone he yet fought, silent except to bark for things he needed. His throaty voice rasped her nerves.

"The water, boy, the milk—" He mumbled, his eyes turning from hers.

"Yes, lord?" She said, stubbornly speaking in Anglish. Her land's brusque tongue hid her feminine voice. And—she shrugged inside—it was better he did not know she could more than understand his Araby tongue.

Gershem was mixed in his mind at times. She was glad he recovered, though mostly for Faisal's sake. Her head ached. But there was something she ought to remember ... her mind was too foggy to recall the Master of the Stars' words. What was it? Something about not letting the sun go down on her anger. Oh, and the milk. Alaina rubbed her forehead and gripped the tent pole a moment.

Gershem rolled over, presenting his back to her. *Burn it!* Her heart screamed in frustration. Her hands tightened—but she did not pick up the pole and whirl it whistling through the air, a staff to fight off her unseen enemies—enemies who pressed in, a red, dangerous tide of resentment. If she did, the edge of the tent would fall. Gershem would rise up in his rugs, shouting obscenities. Alaina's mouth twitched. It might be worth it. She sobered.

Gershem's one servant, young Farook, had been relieved to give his sheyk's care over to Tae, and Tae to her, still in her man's disguise from their flight across the desert. Tae had instructed her to grind the goat's gland fine, to be sure to keep it cool, and to use it for one day only before mixing a new paste. Farook would supply everything she needed.

Then Tae went off to take council at the Oasis with Faisal and Sheyk Shahin and the Aneza. They were free, so much freer than an apprentice scribe, who could not practice. Her mouth twisted again.

Burn it, it was *not* just.

But the world was not just, it was not kind, and often men did not see truly. If she had only woken earlier that morn in the desert, had not leaped up like a scared rabbit startled from its burrow. Faisal had not noticed, had he?

She pursed her lips, torn between the heat in her heart and the tears that pricked her eyes. The prince of the desert's red turban had been as impeccably wound as if he had not slept in it five nights. Nothing was left to him of the waif in the dirty blue turban who attacked her sister seasons agone, or the uncertain man who encouraged them on the way to Jedda and took her message; there was nothing but his wolfish will, revealed in the tightness of his mouth as he gazed back over their trail.

Had Faisal thought her over–delicate when she turned from Truthseeker? It seemed the prince had taken to heart Tae's old lesson about the weight and right of power.

Hot sadness had choked her. She had not wished to see the bird or his face through her veil of tears. The falcon's talons were sharp, and she with no leather or cloth armguard, though a corner of her blanket might have done.

Alaina rested her head against the pole. Kyrin would have taken Truthseeker without a thought for her pierced skin. Alaina sighed. Why did everything look so dark?

She had not truly thought of being included in the Oasis council. Visiting Mey, Shahin's wife, and little Rashid and the other women would have been a pleasant cease from the round of cooking greens in broth, cleaning and tending Gershem, then returning to her tent to be besieged by Twilkets. For the sick in camp had discovered her gift with herbs. Now she donned her robes under her blankets for she never knew when someone would step inside her tent, thinking her a boy.

She was simply tired, or her thoughts would not weigh so heavy. Alaina blew out her breath. She did not mind her supplicants so much; there was nothing better than seeing someone smile after a hurt left them. But Tae had left her with Gershem without a word, and gone to the council. Though he must have his reasons.

The sheyk's tent stank. Alaina made a face. What she would give for a bottle of rosewater. She rubbed her nose on her arm again, feeling like a grimacing monkey. She had better ask Farook for the milk.

Do not let the sun go down on your anger. Across the tent Gershem stirred, restless against his pillows. She needed to tire herself with the swift strength and speed of body and staff, to calm herself before she took up the wood with violence. *Give me strength . . .* She left the pole with an upward glance and a last regretful caress.

§

Faisal spurred Zahir and the horse broke into a gallop, earth flying from his hooves. Faisal ducked the limbs of the junipers, lying flat along the stallion's neck. He had sought news and found it with Alaina and Tae outside Jedda. So he had told the council, standing among them as was his right.

"The wazir raises taxes on every merchant's load of goods that pass through the desert and the gates of the caliph's city. My grandfather's caravanseri and the Oasis of Oaths are known across the northern and southern desert as a meeting place for merchants and trade. From the Far East"—he nodded at Tae— "to the land of bright gold, men the shade of black pepper, and bananas. On top of his tax, which the southernmost Kathirib tribes support, the caliph gives the Kathirib good coin to raid those who do not agree. We may look for danger to come out of the sands." Some in the council circle shook their heads.

Kentar's face was tight as he stood to speak. "You who doubt say we are not yet at war with the wazir, yet he sets our enemies against us. Numerous enemies, whom we will fight when they come with the spring rains. Yet you say we must refuse the caliph's tax. How is this not already war with the wazir and the caliph? You hide your head as the ostrich. One day you will find it parted from your body." With a glare, Kentar sat. Dignified in his anger, as *dalil* and veteran guide of caravans, he now advised his prince. Faisal smiled crookedly at him, and inclined his head to Tae, who had predicted the council's reaction. His mouth quirked.

The wazir, who advised the caliph, blessed be he, had named a worthy price for his enemy. And it was meet, for it was said Tae Chisun could kill with a touch. Faisal did not doubt it. Sirius Abdasir would not be pleased to learn that he, Faisal Ben Salin of the Twilkets, sheltered those he hunted, despite much gold offered. For Tae shook the hearts of men with his martial art of *Subak* and *Taekyon*. Even prince of the Twilkets as Faisal was, *he* would fear Tae if he did not know his heart was true.

A hand touched Faisal's shoulder, and Farook leaned to whisper in his ear. Sheyk Gershem was better. He left Tae and Kentar to debate their opponents and rode, Farook following.

Faisal wove Zahir between the trees about the spreading black dwellings of his people. He wished to see before being seen. There—his grandfather sat in the brightening sun at the edge of camp, his smile broad, eating at Hafiz's fire.

Faisal reined Zahir and slid down. He nodded to Hafiz and sank to the rug beside his grandfather. Cooked lamb and lentils with curry pulled at his nose and tongue. He swallowed. It had been long since last night's fire and food. "Sheyk Gershem, it delights my heart to see you enjoy meat."

"Yes, Faisal, it is good." His grandfather's smile cracked his lean face. "A gift of Allah—and faithful Hafiz." He reached to the platter before his crossed legs and tore away a bit of leg. "Open your hand, my son."

Faisal eyed Hafiz's widening smile but took the meat. Hafiz would not dare move against him while his grandfather lived. As first warrior he gained power through his sheyk's approval. Faisal chewed, the meat dry in his mouth. Hafiz often kept him awake, staring into the dark in his tent at night. When would Hafiz try to rid himself of him? His grandfather would hear no word of his against his first warrior, and no evil about him from Hafiz. Faisal scowled. It was as if they were both the Sheyk's sons, though he was a son's son, and Hafiz without a drop of Gershem's blood, and even less of his spirit.

Though he knew it could not be, the meat tasted of blood. But let Hafiz frown over those who broke the prophet's law. That law was no longer his.

Faisal swallowed his mouthful and rose. "Peace to you. My horse needs the cool pools." He needed it more. Hafiz and his wiles could wait—he would teach him the ruses of the sand fox later.

"The council—what did they decide?" Gershem's dark eyes were expectant. Faisal glanced between his sheyk and Hafiz. His grandfather must know—but Hafiz wished him to say the words of the council's rejection himself. What trap did the first warrior lay? He would not be baited.

"Grandfather, my words are for your ears. What happened, I am sure Hafiz has told you."

Gershem nodded, his mouth rueful, the loose skin of his neck wobbling. "I am sure, my son. Go. Rest, and give your Zahir drink." His shoulders slumped and he stared at the platter before him, an old warrior in troubled times.

Faisal's chest tightened. He knelt and touched the back of Gershem's brown, dry hand. "We will live free, as we always have. Twilket hearts are of one blood with the lion." Gershem's onyx eyes lit. Faisal grinned. "Do not tire yourself; there will be more meat before the stars shine. Sahar and I will seek you a plump sand hen."

Gershem nodded eagerly. Hafiz's eyes narrowed and his mouth twisted as if on sour milk. *Hyena.* Faisal let his teeth show, and swung away.

After he watered Zahir, would Alaina find pleasure in a hunt up the mountain where a falcon once sought her eyrie, and Truthseeker had come from the egg? His hand closed on Zahir's saddle. But Alaina yet remembered he had pursued her sister's blood at that time. Did she and Kyrin still name him *jackal?* Those who carried lances among his people called him many things. *Twilket prince, betrayer of Allah, weak follower of Jesu, desert wolf. Jackal,* it might be.

What was he? A man—caught in a web he could not fight free of. As he mounted he muttered, "The Master of the Stars rules, and teaches men to rule themselves. To grow—a most hard task." *Ahh, Jesu, I fall into such tangles.*

But even if Alaina frowned at him, she would not bury a blade in his back. And a hunt had to be better than grinding herbs and goat innards, and cooking and cleaning platters. The wind in one's face always whispered of freedom, however short it might be. He found his way to the open side of Gershem's black tent and called, "Sarni?"

A shadow within stirred and straightened. Alaina came into the light, squinting, pulling at her kaffiyeh that she had wound and tucked up into a turban in the manner of Oman. She did not protest the name he gave her. Her braid of red-gold thumped perversely down, and she tucked it back under her kaffiyeh with quick fingers, glancing around him and his horse for watchers. She let out her breath and straightened her shoulders.

Suddenly in an expansive mood, Faisal smiled. "The sun is rising, and it is good for my grandfather. Why do you not lift the sides of the tent? The air will take away the stink." That same sun blazed in her hair in dark golden glory.

Her near-hazel gaze rose to his, her lips thinning. "He claims the light hurts his eyes." There was a mulish cant to her shoulders.

Faisal frowned. "You are the healer, are you not?"

"And what of that?" Her kaffiyeh waved against her cheek, coming undone again. Her hands clenched. "Am I his mother or your slave, to order him about or to leap at your word?"

"I did not mean to anger you—"

"Well, what do you wish?"

"Truthseeker was taken from the nest, up there." He motioned at the mountain flanks, thick with juniper and scattered fig. "Kyrin—" He floundered. "She would—"

"What? What would she do? Cook and clean and slave for you until you gave her another falcon? A falcon that strikes with beak and talon, with a gaze that searches out trouble? I'd rather a desert lark. Its song would at least sweeten the sun's rising."

Faisal raised an eyebrow. "Kyrin would never—"

"No," Alaina choked. "I'm not her. Don't you understand? Don't your eyes see? I'm not her. I'm not—Kyrin—and I don't want to be!"

Not like Kyrin? He wanted to laugh. Alaina sacrificed for others, nursed a stranger who had been her enemy. She was more like Kyrin than she knew. But why the sudden disavowal of her sister? "Why don't you wish so?"

Alaina glared. "You ask—in this hot, dusty, lampless place? I haven't seen a quill or a parchment since I came to this tent. I go from Gershem's side to tend your people before my door, to eat cold meat and dates, and fall onto my blanket and rug. Men walk in and out of—of Sarni's tent—as they wish. A scribe is worthless in this place. As is my staff. I have not even read from the Book this past seven-day." Her hands clenched tight, she quivered, and her breath came quick.

Why was she afraid? "Have any treated you ill?" Faisal asked carefully. She and Tae were under the protection of his tent. Had Hafiz spoken to her? He should have had Farook watch her, too. Though she could wield the staff she carried, there were other ways for one determined to kill her: poison, a fall, a stray hoof or camel-pad of a maddened beast. He frowned again.

He would not have her voice stilled, though it was far from a lark's this moment. His laughter fell completely away. Hafiz would attack Tae first or think better of his oath of Nur-ed-Dam. Tae was not a threat to leave at one's back. If harm came to Alaina . . .

Her eyes blazed hot and green, as if in answer to his fierce thoughts. "No—I have not been treated ill—unless you count leaving me to care for your sheyk as if I were a concubine. While you and Tae go to council, to hear and decide our course. No one has come near me but Farook. I believed I was a slave no longer."

"Ah." She felt powerless. He slid down from his horse and cleared his throat. "Did you know my people hold Tae Chisun in awe? My grandfather's men yet tell the tale of the night the strange warrior came to the sheyk's tent. They followed him out of camp, waiting to kill him. He escaped them and faced our sheyk the following sun, to tell of each man's fault in stealth to his face." Faisal grinned. "Hafiz breathed too loud, and the feathers of another man's arrows rustled in his quiver. Tae could have killed them that night. Then he stood on the sand, under threat of Twilket torture, and bearded our sheyk on his horse—before them all."

"And then Gershem tried to kill him—and Tae pulled your grandfather from the saddle in a breath and put a blade to his throat." There was triumph in Alaina's tone and challenge in her eyes.

"Yes." He inclined his head. "Hafiz and many others thought Tae had the help of Djinn. They think so still." He let out his breath. "So no, none of us interferes with Tae Chisun or his apprentice, called Sarni." His mouth flattened. *Not while anyone watches. Though Hafiz has sworn the oath of blood, Nur-ed-Dam, against all with even a distant hand in his uncle's death. Thank Jesu, Kyrin Cieri is gone from his reach.*

Alaina's graceful hand seemed drawn to her dangling kaffiyeh, fruitlessly trying to tuck it into place.

Faisal continued quietly, "You are no slave, but I thought it best not to have too many nearby to discover your secret, Sarni. The fewer arrows Hafiz finds in my brothers' mouths that concern me, the fewer he may shoot. The council"—he shrugged—"it was more a task of many words thrown against closed ears. Be glad you were not there to have your ears assaulted."

Alaina crossed her arms. "I would have the choice to decide what assault my ears bear—and what wearies them." Her cheeks reddened and she looked aside. "Here, there is no caliph, and yet no freedom."

His neck heated. Stubborn girl. "What would you have then?"

She glanced up and her mouth trembled. Frustration stiffened it. "I want to speak life—to speak and write things that matter." She glared at him again. "I can, you know."

"Speak life?" He watched her closely.

She flung out her hands. "Don't you know? A people's stories, their words—they carry meaning, deep meaning. What courage a people honors, what truths they cling to, what evils they fight. These words shape us: speak of our life—or our death. I want to speak and write of life. But that will not happen here," she whispered. "This place is empty." She waved at the tents around them. "Nothing of import happens here, in the dust, herding camels and goats . . ." She trailed off at his impassive face, looked down, and gripped her arms tighter. She swallowed. "I should not have spoken so, but I have not seen a quill or my staff in long and long. I am sorry. I have been thinking ill thoughts. Everyone's story is gold to them—I just meant—in Baghdad . . . well, I could write Kyrin's tale and there would be ears to listen. They might favor what they heard and give me greater things to write. Of their city, or it may be, even of the caliph. Forgive me." She turned toward the tent's inner gloom, and her low mutter drifted back. "Burn it, it's done now."

Faisal laughed low. She had spirit enough for two, caged in his grandfather's tent, with the prickles of a rolled hedgehog.

She glanced back, suspicious, her shoulders hunched. "What?"

"Come." He handed Zahir's rein to a worried Farook, who hovered behind him, and beckoned her closer. He wrinkled his nose. She smelled of spoilt milk and goat. Did she not bathe? There was much water in the wadi—had she truly so few moments to care for herself? He smoothed the grimace from his face and led her toward the edge of camp. Under a thick juniper, he threw back the flap of his small tent.

Alaina stepped inside and her foot caught on the edge of the thick red rug. She stumbled. Faisal dared not steady her. She would not welcome his touch.

Wood shelves lined two sides of the tent, stacked deep with scrolls, parchments, and papers. Mouth slightly open, her eyes alight, Alaina drew her fingers along the wood below the top row on the left.

Faisal suppressed his smile. His knee-high Persian table stood on their right, fat cushions about it. On its polished wood top rested his bottle of ink and a holder with three quills. One white, one black, and one dyed red. His hand tightened at his side.

The red feather quill he'd dyed on a night when Hafiz pressed him hard. John's first letter lay beside it on the table, the scroll held open by smooth stones laid at the edges. He remembered the last line before the next scroll. *There is no fear in love, but perfect love casts out fear.* A father's love, yes. A lover's? He did not know. But what made him think of that? Humans were fallible; they never loved perfectly.

He tapped the dagger in his sash. Alaina's eyes jumped to the weapon then to his face. She could not fear his strength—what then? She feared him, or something about him.

"How—who uses this?" She touched the quill and took a step away from him.

He smiled gently at her astonishment. "I often have need to scribe messages."

She looked at him and her gaze narrowed.

He grinned. "From the street to leading men through the desert, I never lost my taste for words. My master in Gaza— where you and Kyrin found me—he had many books, though he was a spice merchant with many camels. He had his overseer instruct me to read because he saw how my eyes darkened at the thought. It was the foolishess of a child. Those words gave me cities and kingdoms, men's hearts and truth. As you say, they mean much." Change had always followed him. Her sash was blue, as robin's-egg blue as his turban had been then, though infinitely cleaner. Whether he studied or did his household tasks that blue had gathered stains from one rising of the sun to the next. He had worn it on the street in defiance. "Later, I understood he wished me to learn the riches that words hold. Truly, they broke my bonds." He dared look at her. "The merchant died, and his son, who loved him ill, cast me out. I never gave my master thanks. Now I read the Book and histories of war and other lands. Many men have faced the things I see before me. That . . . is good to know."

His gaze shifted to her face. "Tae tells me that those of Ali's house knew you for your poetry. Though we have no great deeds here, I would read your words, if you will write some." He swallowed, knowing he nattered on worse than a grey-hair. "I beg you, don't speak of it to my grandfather. He feels my—taste—for words led to my serving your Master of the crossed trees."

"No. I won't speak of it." She hesitated. "I—I may come here, and use this—place?"

"Yes. Take paper and ink as you wish. I may require your quill." He would think of something for her to write. "My people will not forbid you. They yet acknowledge my word, though they are not of one heart in it." He grimaced.

Her chin lifted, fire beginning in her eyes. What made her so prickly? He had no time for feelings stirred by every breath of wind; his people did not. In this she must see the truth of where they were placed, just as he must face it. Faisal closed his eyes, opened them, and said in a hard voice, "Sheyk Gershem of the Twilkets will pass from us, and with him his line of rule, though he wishes otherwise." His fingers found the red-feathered quill and brushed back, against the soft edges, savaging them. The ride up the mountain beside her was as far away as if it had never been. "Our elders serve Allah—though they give me honor as long as I show sufficient—wolfishness." His voice lowered.

"Divided wills among them would shatter my rule. They know my heart on this; I have told them I do not wish strife or the death of any of them. The Kathirib seek our lands. They think us threatened by the wazir's reach, though we keep Umar at bay, sending him around the outer camps, searching for you and Tae."

Alaina said nothing.

He clenched the tattered feather in his fist and his nostrils flared. "I will not let anyone drag my people down to death. I will see Hafiz and those like him, who desire sheep for their jaws, crushed. Power gives no man the right to challenge another. Our Master of the Stars' command to do righteousness gives me the right to oppose Hafiz, since his word has placed me here. I cannot abandon my people—though the mountains and the desert do not seek my blood as some of them do, with malice. All who seek me will find a wolf." His fierceness tugged at his face.

Not for him the life of a simple warrior, gaining glory with lance and dagger. Not for him the pleasure of knowing his father's line lived. He would be sheyk and lead men who looked to him in a desperate war. He would care for the tents of those who did not love him. And then he would go. He would go to the mountains.

Her eyes wary, her mouth taught, Alaina stepped back, feeling behind her for the wood shelf of scrolls.

"You need not fear me." Inside him something wished her to, wished someone would count him worthy of caution. He schooled his face, smoothed the bedraggled feather, laid it in her hand, and turned his back. She was not Hafiz, she would not bear his hard words, destined for another. But they choked him.

The black felt wall rippled beside him. They both jumped. Sahar's red muzzle nudged beneath. She slipped to his side with a low whine and rested a heavy paw on his foot. Faisal drew a breath and held it, closing his eyes. Sahar always seemed to know when he was about to break.

Alaina's voice was low but clear. "I used to hate you, you know, for my sister."

He forced a smile, and turned. He must turn from his lurking bitterness for Hafiz. His bleakness cast shadows.

"Kyrin did not wish you pain, but her pillow was often wet. You—" She hesitated, and straightened her shoulders. "You stirred doubts in her that she battled hard. Did you know she had evil dreams? A chained falcon—and a tiger. She fought the beast often and tried to free the falcon. She would shake beside me in fear and anger and wake crying out." Alaina's whisper sank away.

Faisal stared at her. He had not known, and his heart twisted. His wry, almost bitter laugh surprised them both. "Did *you* know I loved her? She carried a dangerous light, a bright flame in the desert night. And was I a moth—for all my striving to be a lion. Then she left me. And that light pursued me—it burned away the lion's hide I hid in. I found myself a man, naked, without teeth or claws, as my creator made me." Sahar shoved her nose under his hand.

Alaina glanced from him to Sahar with a growing smile.

He sobered. Ought he to tell her what Tae saw ahead for them? No, it was not the moment. Better if she came to the knowledge herself.

It was too much to ask that she welcome leaving her green land and all she had known in Ali's house: the courts, the food, the certainty of seeing one day after another. At least, as certain as one could be on this earth. She did smile at Sahar. No. The mountain would have to wait.

4

Word and Weapon

Thy word I have treasured in my heart. ~ Psalm 119:11

Tae returned from the council and caravanseri at the Oasis of Oaths with greetings for Alaina from Sheyk Shahin, Mey, and Rashid, who were well. He spent the following days with Gershem's men, teaching unarmed combat to those who wished it. Hafiz was among the first to step forward. Most of the rest of the sheyk's warriors followed him, intensely interested.

Hearing the shouts and the thud of flesh on wood, the squeak and clash of weapons in the dawn, Alaina ached to spar with Tae, to work through the familiar patterns, her staff whistling through the air, thrumming in her hand, clacking against his. Since that could not be, instead she often sought Faisal's scribe tent and occupied herself with words. Besides outlining Kyrin's Chronicle, she recorded recent Aneza history where her sister had changed its course. That day, the sides of the tent opposite the shelves were propped up to let in the breeze. Outside, she saw Faisal stroding from fire to fire, his *bisht* swirling behind him.

Doubtless he spoke of the gathering Kathirib in the south, and of Sirius, who had lent his red-cloaked warriors to the Kathirib ranks to instruct nearby tribes who did not wish to heed the wazir's word. The unrest among the caliph's guard in Baghdad had been quelled by two more executions.

Alaina wondered if the wazir would disrupt the sworn peace and trade among the tribes that Tae and Kentar had gathered under Ali's command years ago, trade agreements that held firm despite Ali's treachery. Kentar, Tae's unofficial eyes, ears, and emissary between Ali and the tribes, had somehow kept the bond of far-flung trade whole after Ali's execution. Would the tribes' oath stand the strain of her and Tae, hunted as they were by the wazir, the man who walked closest to the caliph? She dated the entry and her quill paused. Only if Kentar's trade contacts in the ports and towns held firm could they gain news of the wazir's movements. Umar's Hand proved tenacious.

They needed news of that Hand if they were to foil the wazir—news of him who made himself their enemy. Did Seliam fight with Sirius's red-cloaked warriors and the Kathirib in the sands, or had the wazir kept him close to lead his guard? When his men came to instruct the tribes in the error of their ways, would Sirius Abdasir crush her and Tae with the Aneza and Twilkets? Once bitter enemies, they had come to peace. But the caliph could destroy the Oasis of Oaths, stop up the spring, salt the earth, cut down the date palms—and most in the desert would spit on his name. Many in the cities would spit without speaking.

Alaina's grip threatened to break the quill in her fingers. Umar would find them. There were only so many tents to search, so many camps across the desert, even if she and Tae left Faisal's tents to hide and returned after the Kathirib left.

Many would die under Kathirib lances. Those who lived would retreat into the sands, the hills, and the mountains. Nomads in their own desert lands, well used to changing boundaries, they would fight a war from hiding, with skill. Faisal and his men would strike as the hyena, disemboweling the trade caravans until they brought the routes down by loss of blood, and more painful to the caliph, loss of coin. Trade would cost more, and goods increase.

Kyrin, as you love us, please find Hamal quickly.

Winter passed, and Umar did not find them. Gershem recovered a measure of strength but stayed near the warm fires and tents and fat cushions. Alaina found fewer supplicants at her door and those only in the morn after she broke fast. She was grateful. From the covert glances of some of the women she rather thought some of them knew her secret, but none said a word. As if what was not spoken, did not exist.

Suns rose and fell into starlight. The spring flush of chamomile nodded in a delicate carpet above the sand. Too soon, the lush camel thorn and thin grasses shuddered and browned. At the edge of the great sands they shriveled into dust. The desert heat sucked away every drop of moisture; tortured man, beast, and rock alike. Alaina shrank inside at the blazing expanse, but was glad of it for one reason.

The gathering Kathirib would skirt the desert after the land cooled. The days of summer saw their frustration, for the sands were near impassable and the hills inhospitable to a large force. All waited. One thing comforted her. The tribes of Yemen, who occupied the most fertile, productive ground, grew much incense, and refused to allow the caliph's forces through their mountains. Even the wazir hesitated to force their hand. The Kathirib would not attack from there.

Faisal began to take longer hunts with Sahar and one or two men. Most often Kentar, Youbib, or Tae. Alaina suspected they scouted. When needed, Farook took messages to Shahin and the other Aneza sheyks, while Kentar brought word to and from merchants and those who were the deserts' eyes and ears in the ports and towns. Tae advised on warfare and diplomacy and guarded Faisal's back.

As Alaina followed Tae and assisted him with herbal matters, she listened closely to any talk she overheard about the prince. Faisal knew little of courtly words, of the nuances of poisonous tongues, of the art of drawing away a rival's supporters and showing him in the worst light. Hafiz was a master at it. Alaina snorted. The prince ignored his barbs. Sarni was often angered. Sometimes, she wished she were in Farook's place. In a position close to Faisal, as Sarni she could speak subtly for the prince, weaken Hafiz's attacks, tear down his fortresses of words.

But Faisal spoke little with her. Her prince reminded her of a caged wolf, pacing within invisible walls of rejection and fear, of expectation and indifference that hemmed him in. If only he might be freed. To her disappointment he had not yet called for her quill or her verses. Kneeling at his table in his tent, Alaina sighed. He would have to speak to her at some point. Burn it all, anyway.

She smoothed the feather of his red, bedraggled quill. Its curve and color most often lent itself to her hand. She pressed her lips together. This moment her mind was blank, her heart too heavy to write any verse, without Faisal. Well, he would have to wait, since he'd forgotten. She would trust and wait.

Ah. She could begin Kyrin's history, as the outline was finished. It would keep her hand in trim and darker things at bay. Faisal's face filled her mind as she bent to her work. His expression this morning had been terrible, so strong in its struggle for hope. Then Hafiz descended, and Faisal left. What was hope but holding on in the face of fear, holding on to the rock that was higher than they?

Paper from the East was expensive. Alaina shoved the stack of sheets back and drew on a pile of less costly parchment. The quill's feather tickled her chin as she mused, and she spared a caress for Cicero's warm head in her lap. He sighed, content. Content or not, she must to work.

As Kyrin's scribe, what was she? A bard, a minstrel? Her voice could hardly compare to the thunder of the bards in her land, and she'd never touched a harp.

Scop. She was Kyrin's Scop. That old name those of the hills called the one who kept and fed the flame of a tribe's feats in love and life and war, the one who brought their deeds alive with all the might of head and heart and hand. Scop. Her sister's deeds would be written for any to read who would. The caliph's court little deserved them, if they thought only of poetry. Nimah and Nara and some of the women of Ali's house would rejoice over it. But first it must be written. Alaina bent over her parchment.

Scop's Chronicle, Book One. That would fit. For Kyrin held the heart of a falcon—friend against foe, love against treachery. *Falcon and tiger—dagger and sword. A falcon's heart. Yes. The Falcon Chronicle.* That fit better.

When her hand cramped over the Chronicle, Alaina wrote scraps of Faisal's words on another parchment, for his conflict echoed in her head. Beside them she put bits of encouragement that welled up in her in answer.

That light . . . burned away the lion's hide I hid in. Careful and slow, she penned, *Thy Word is a lamp unto my feet and a light to my path.* She rubbed her forehead. What was it he'd said? Something like, *I cannot abandon my people—though the mountains and the desert do not seek my blood with malice.* She nodded. He needed a sword against the lies that plagued him. She pushed the nib of his red quill scratching across the parchment, displacing emptiness. *The word is sharper than a two-edged sword, piercing between soul and spirit, judging the thoughts and intentions of the heart . . .*

Farook stepped inside the tent and glanced about for Faisal. Alaina slid Kyrin's history over the parchment with Faisal's words. Farook nodded to her and ducked back out.

He, like Faisal, did not speak to her often. Whether he and his prince had things to do, or were discomfited by her presence, to her joy, Cicero slept at her feet at night.

By day he romped under the sun with Sahar, whose reddish coat fit her name—the dawn. Once, in the early light before Gershem's dark tent, the salukis ran side by side, their slender legs kicking up earth. Sahar's long-furred tail and ears streamed in the wind of their speed. They stopped short and circled each other, regal heads almost touching, somehow hesitant. The rising sun gilded both Cicero's short, shadow-moon touched fur, and Sahar's blazing red. They touched noses and loped into the trees.

Watching from Gershem's door, Faisal had shaken his head. She thought his mouth twitched. When she smiled at him, the prince turned away. Alaina had frowned at his back.

It was a good day to smile at another, to walk beside a fellow human being, war or no war. Why had he begun to avoid her? Or was he avoiding instead a message he must write but did not want to face? Surely he did not avoid her. He *had* sent Farook to her with a brown mare of agile stock.

The morning before, she'd woken to a whinny at her door. Opening the tent flap, she had laid her hand instinctively on the mare's nose when she startled. The horse quieted, and Alaina cried low after the servant, not to wake those nearby, "Farook, wait! What is she called?"

He turned in mid-step and looked at his feet. "That is for you to say, Sarni."

Alaina stared at him, her mouth open. Sarni again—elevated one. Had Faisal told him to call her so? Everyone else did, and she was not sure if she should be angry or pleased. But a desert prince gave her a horse, though he would not speak to her, and the mare's dark eye was friendly.

Farook served Faisal. He would not give her away if he discovered her secret. Her name was safe from him. She inclined her head. "I thank you, Farook. I am most well pleased."

Farook had drawn himself up with a proud smile and walked away.

Alaina sighed and stroked Cicero again. She missed the women's garden, Nara and her cakes, and Zoltan's harmless mischief in Ali's household. Most of all, her thoughts turned to Nimah. Had Nimah found a secure place in Ali's erstwhile house, now the wazir's? Had she taken her parting words to heart and worked her artistry with a needle on one of Sirius Abdasir's thawbs? Had he seen its worth?

Of the women yearning to know how Alaina designed Ali's sumptuous clothing, Nimah had applied herself to Alaina's teaching the most. A robe that accented a graceful form, design and color that complemented the wearer, whose elements did not clash with henna patterns; these things made Nimah's face glow with smiles. Her embroidery had no rival and her tongue no equal. Though she possessed the voice of a nightingale, she knew when to hold her peace and when to speak, and might be an unparalleled source of news in the wazir's household. She had a natural gift for creating beauty—all the more to quiet suspicion. Alaina pursed her mouth. She would mention Nimah to Tae. She shook herself—she had better attend to her own gifts before they withered away. *Healer, see to thyself.*

Before the sun set, Alaina rode the mare to the wadi at the foot of the mountain. She went again the following dawn. At last she could bring her staff.

Quiet graced the worn stone hollows of the wadi bed. The pools held good, sweet water, though green with moss, unlike the clear spring of the Oasis of Oaths. Alaina dismounted and drank a little. She wiped her mouth and tied her mare's rein to an ancient olive branch. The water tasted rather of green.

Her body ached with the stiffness and tension of the last few days. She moved from a walk to swift trot, and at last broke into a run, staff in hand. Behind an arm of the mountain, in a space among the junipers, it was private enough to practice. And oh joy, she could take off her kaffiyeh.

Breathing hard from her run, she loosened her hair, shaking it over her shoulders. The wind was fresh. No need to tie her hair back, she was not after blood this morn. Alaina breathed deep. The junipers had their own incense. It was cool in the shaded valley. Juniper needles and duff crackled under her feet. The staff was solid in her hand. She grinned.

She would spar with Kyrin, who she could just imagine facing her in a shaft of light streaming between an olive and a juniper. Kyrin's small smile dared her to do her worst, and her eyes laughed. A challenge had been cast; Alaina laughed in return. "I'll get you! Burn you yet!" Memories of Kyrin spilled into her mind, glittering like jewels.

She sparred and drilled in the cool sunlight until she was shaking and sore, and, after a dip in the pool, returned to her tent for milk and dates. Her quill waited for her.

Alaina sat at Faisal's scribe table, her wet hair spread over her shoulders to dry. In caution, she'd closed the tent. Cicero padded to her side and sat bolt upright on her left, and she spared a hand to rub behind his ears. Sahar joined them, flanking her. Alaina looked at her. "Won't your master miss you?" Sahar flattened her ears a little and her tail thumped the rug. "Well, I suppose you may stay." Sahar licked her hand in gratitude.

Sometime later, Alaina's fingers were cramped about the quill when the tent flap rustled. Faisal brushed it aside, stepped in, and stopped, staring at her. She froze, staring back at him. Behind him, the shadows lengthened.

Horrified, Alaina said, "My pardon, I did not mean to stay so long. I lost myself in the words—"

But Faisal scowled, his gaze on Sahar. "*There* you are. Since you missed the hunt before the sun we need a gazelle for the night fire." Sahar paced to his side with a happy *whip, whip* of her tail, and looked over her shoulder with a whine. Cicero lifted his head from Alaina's lap and trotted to her side. Faisal shrugged and raised his eyebrows in question. With a quirk of her mouth and a breath of relief, Alaina tilted her head in permission toward the door. It would be good for Cicero to run.

Faisal eyed her hair, his bisht dark about his wide shoulders, blending with the juniper trunk's shadow outside, evening light spearing through the branches to weave golden lace across his side. Then he was gone. But he had spoken to her.

Alaina sighed, arched her back, and rubbed at the knot in her neck. Her hair had dried, and a ride on the mare would be heaven, though she had not yet found her a name. Frowning, she stared at the cup of milk near her hand. Maybe in the morn. Kyrin's Chronicle waited for no man, and Hafiz was equally impatient.

Alaina left Kyrin's Chronicle in her tent, then went in search of the mare. She could at least brush her. Tae met them at the edge of the sands. When Alaina mentioned her fear of Hafiz, he shook his head. "There is hate there that will not die." Tae's mouth was solemn, the wrinkles about his eyes weary. "Hafiz has sworn Nur-ed-Dam, Alaina, and not revoked his claim, though the elders have. You witnessed the assassin fall in dishonor. Though it was Faisal's hand that took his uncle, it was Kyrin's blade. Hafiz has not forgotten. He knows who carried the blade, and blames her. Though he may not know about Faisal's blow against his blood. Be careful of him."

Alaina licked her lips. *Hafiz will* never *know if I have anything to say about it.* "I will be careful, Tae. But I'm not without strength."

"No, yet the strongest woman should beware the strength of a man and the place and mind that give him opportunity to harm." Tae's face was stern.

The strongest woman—a woman such as Kyrin. Or a man such as Faisal, who had killed with honor, to protect, and his tribe accepted him. Who was she to them, an untried scribe?

Alaina swallowed and ducked her head. Hafiz could pierce her disguise should she get close enough to him. He watched those who stood near Faisal closely. And she was not as strong as some. But if she knew the death touch— "Tae . . ."

"Yes?" He was patient. The white about his ear gleamed.

"If I must kill—"

"There will be no need. I and the prince have seen to it. You will be beyond their reach." He came near and touched her shoulder. "I know you practice, and I am glad. But you are safe, if you do not tempt Hafiz. Soon you will be beyond him. If he values his life."

Alaina shook her head in bewilderment. "Are we leaving?" She would be alone again. Was she not his daughter also? She wished Tae would put his arm around her. "I won't go without you."

"No, we are not leaving. You will see, but it is better we do not speak of it yet. Avoid Hafiz for the time, and all will be well."

"What if the Kathirib send men or Umar comes in the night? Any of them could force me to defend myself. With the death touch I could stop them."

Tae studied her. "You have enough to do tending Gershem and the ill, and growing in skill with your staff. Though hand to hand a man's strength is greater, you can best any three men with a bit of wood. Be it a pestle as long as your hand, such a weapon evens your battleground. You should not fear."

Alaina flushed. He thought she feared? No, she wanted to bring down what threatened Faisal, what threatened them all. Burn it, even if they did not let her speak in council, she could use what Tae taught Kyrin—but he did not think she needed it. Had the sun blinded him?

"Tae, those in this camp who know me as Sarni do not hear me. My words are dust to them. I—I want to help. I can't wait for war and do nothing. I can write messages for you and speak with those about the fires, walk with you, help you teach—mayhap the women. Please . . ."

Tae squeezed her shoulder. "You feel alone?"

"No—yes." He didn't understand. The sweat of his day's practice wafted to her. "Kyrin left on her journey, and she will fight." Alaina faced him. "I can fight, too."

Tae gripped her shoulders. "I know, my daughter," he whispered, "I know you can. But it is not necessary."

Alaina gulped back hot tears. Burn them. "The death touch—"

"That is not for you." His voice was low and hard. "You will not be forced to such. If necessary, Faisal will challenge Hafiz's Nur-ed-Dam himself, though he does not wish his blood."

"Would Hafiz be satisfied? Would he stop seeking our blood, Kyrin's blood? I am strong enough to learn it—"

"No, trust me, my daughter." He kissed her forehead. "It is not something to wish for, the touch of death." He held her close.

Alaina sighed and slumped into his steady warmth. Did he fear for Faisal as she did? The prince did not raid with the Kathirib so close, but Hafiz did. The men followed him gladly.

Trade brought life to the incense route, to caravanseri and oasis: the East's silk, paper, and ink; Persian tables, tableware, and trousers; Araby's sea pearls, camel leather, and rose perfume from the mountains. Such trade was life to every Twilket, even to Faisal's men, torn between him and Hafiz. Trade, and raiding. Alaina frowned in thought.

"Might I at least send a letter to Kyrin? Tell her how things are with us? Kentar could take it to Kaish and the *Sabra.* And pass our news to Nimah, if she is in charge of the wazir's robing, as I told her Qadira's preference. Nimah will know much if she gained that place. She can speak to Zoltan, who will carry important news outside the house on his hunts, to Kentar. So to us, and we will learn of the wazir's schemes."

Tae's face lit. "A good thought, daughter, a worthy thought. We have news from elsewhere, but none from Sirius's household." He smiled at her. "You have a mind to catch snakes at their own work. It will be done. And the time is right. You will help Faisal much, if you will it."

The time was right for what? Her mouth firmed. "I do mean to help the prince. Hafiz is not just, he nips and chases at Faisal's heels, alluding to his dishonor."

Tae's glance turned grim. "Listen to Hafiz and learn the tricks of those around him. But beware their hearts."

"I will." Alaina smiled. Her mouth trembled. She could do more. She could defend him. "Gershem's men, they do not know the worth of their prince."

"No." Tae looked at the ground, a sad curve about his mouth. "It is often so. Faisal will need us; he will need you. When the moment comes, be his friend."

5

The Hunt

His heart gathers wickedness. ~ Psalms 41:6

The Twilket and Aneza would meet their enemies in the open desert with horse and lance, courage and guile. If the battle went ill they had the means to fade into the dunes and lead the Kathirib from his people and into trap after trap. Tae Chisun was a master strategist and tactician, skills not often found together—the long and the short ways of battle.

Faisal closed his eyes. The moment had come. He reached for his red quill. It was not in the holder. He took another.

Quick footsteps approached, and beside him, Sahar growled. Faisal touched his dagger and laid a hand on Sahar's head. She quieted.

It was Farook who dashed inside, panting. "My prince, Hafiz makes mock, he has words of yours"—he gulped—"that bare your treacherous heart, or so he boasts."

"My treacherous words? What do you speak of?"

"I—I know not. I ran for you—you will teach them that these honorless words to a Nasrany woman cannot be yours."

As Faisal neared Hafiz's tent, Farook beside him, laughter from many throats sounded within. Faisal stopped and gave the rumpled white quill in his hand to Farook, who tucked it in his sash. The prince walked inside, his back straight. When he came out his face was tight, a flush under his dark skin. He said through clenched teeth, "Where is Alaina—I mean Sarni?"

§

Alaina bit her lip. After the humiliation of the red quill—how was she to know Faisal used the red ink for his most important documents—she would use it one last time. No one could mistake part of her Falcon Chronicle for this.

They'd laughed at her account of Faisal, at an Arab prince lovesick over a foreign unbeliever, a *Nasrany.*

She shook her head. Farook's tongue had loosened when she cornered him at last in the scribe tent. "Their faces were as long as your mare's when my prince offered to hear Hafiz's words to see if they might be his. When Hafiz's stopped shouting, he said, 'I was young and acted in dishonor. I did not know my name was Twilket, then. But I did not write those words.' All could tell he had not, he reddened so at the reading. Some of the men scowled at Hafiz and muttered of slander in their beards." Farook shrugged. "Our prince challenged Hafiz to a hunt for the reem, that he might show him he was no longer a beardless boy. He also said he gave you the use of his pens, for he had need of a scribe. But—his face darkened when he read this." Farook held out the bundle that was her Chronicle. "The prince asks that you use the white quill for such writing. The red is for greater things."

Alaina had nodded, shoving down a flash of anger, grateful she had not had to face the laughing warriors, or a wrathful prince. "I—I am sorry."

"It is but a grain of sand to the prince."

So why had Faisal gone back to avoiding her, and now refuse to look at her? Did he hope to head off wagging tongues by pretending he had little to do with her? Alaina bit her lip. That would be futile. Better he faced their words.

She was glad she had left a blank space in the Chronicle for the matter of the Twilket assassin, and had not written that story, though the war was over. If Hafiz had seen that . . . she slept in a Twilket camp. But this missive was important enough to warrant the the red ink.

The words of Kyrin's letter came to her quickly, the ink smooth and bright as blood. Alaina scraped away the last line from the parchment with the small dagger for the purpose, hesitated, and rewrote, *When will I not need to be protected? Am I so different? I must be strong.* She need never hide her heart from Kyrin.

§

Umar stepped quiet as a leopard behind the rug seller's booth. The owner of the deep purple and blue-dyed rugs had chosen a shaded, stone-paved corner in front of his shop to display his wares so that the sun might not steal the royal colors and the dust might not dim them. The man he had come to find watched the bustling souk of the port of Jedda with a jaundiced eye.

Kaish had risen in the world since he carried the news of the Nasrany who sailed on the *Sabra* and the wazir's task. Now he sold prize goods and netted news in the great market, framed on four sides by brick-walled, double-story shops. A date-brown beard flecked with ash-grey wagged over his white robe, and his sash was brown silk. He stroked a thick, blue woolen rug on his booth-top with a wrinkled hand. Thin streets, the arteries of the city, carried its life to and fro before him. Kaish continued stroking, watching, muttering to himself.

What he said Umar could not hear over the general din of the buyers and sellers of the great souk, each with a booth under an awning or a space in the open air.

Kaish paused. Umar followed his gaze across the men and women milling in the afternoon heat that radiated up from the flagstones until it settled on another dignified face, aged and weathering. Kentar.

Umar stiffened. His back to them, Kentar argued with a seller of saffron and spices, with a gesture of disgust. Umar had but a moment. He touched Kaish's back.

Kaish screeched as a rooster destined for the pot and spun. Kentar glanced over his shoulder toward the booth, and with a smooth step Umar put Kaish between him and Kentar. "Quiet, fool!" He sank down to sit casually out of sight. He had not expected to find Kentar here, not yet. He motioned to Kaish to put away the rug. Kaish strode back into his shop, glaring daggers at Umar, who followed. Inside, Umar rose to his full height. He hated crawling. He brushed dust from his thawb. "Our master wishes to know if the one he seeks has come."

"No, no. Not yet." Kaish's voice was breathy from his fright.

"But Kentar, the dalil, he may carry news." Umar smiled.

Kaish drew himself up, offended. "I know those who ride between the tribes, the villages, and the city with news—I serve all my brothers—as I am paid."

"And if that one trades in treachery to the most blessed?"

Kaish paled and his throat bobbed. "Then the dalil will find his death at your Hand."

"Soon, it will be decided." Umar pressed a small bundle of cloth into his hands. "Give him this—for the guests of the Wolf of the Twilkets. Ask what news you may carry for him. Find out what you can, the caliph is most curious about those Kentar serves. Go." He jerked his head toward the door.

Kaish handled the bundle of grey silk as if it were an egg. Umar peered after him, again crouching behind the booth. A laugh or two followed Kaish as he slipped between men and booths. He stopped beside Kentar, who bent his head to hear him. After some moments the two returned, Kaish chattering as they came. "It has been long since I saw you, dalil. You looked for me, across the way, when an old friend thought to surprise this man of the market." Kaish cackled. "As you see, Allah has seen fit that I sell fish on the docks no more. But coin has crossed my palm with news for you." He gave him the bundle and Umar's message.

"When did you get this?" Kentar's hands tightened on the grey silk convulsively, and he stared into every shadow around the market, and peered into the shop. Umar tensed on the floor. Kaish was a double fool if he contemplated betrayal.

"Why, last night." Kaish spread his hands. "If you wished to speak with the wazir's Hand, I sorrow. The camel boy said he and his Hand of noble ones journey with a caravan bound for the city of the exalted caliph. But he may stop by Makkah, the holy city, or Taif of the mountains. The first rains have blessed them with goods." He shrugged. "But have you news I may send?" His eyes sharpened under his brows and he rubbed his hands together.

Kentar's seamed face was unreadable. He tossed an edge of his green cloak over a dusty shoulder and dug into his sash. "I have a small thing for your hand." A bag clinked.

Kaish beamed. "All know your name is honorable. No news there!" Ah, clever on behalf of his skin. Umar could admire that. Kaish said, "Come, what news of the Wolf who defies the jackal over his prey in the desert?" Kentar stared at him, and the rug-seller continued, "I must hear all, for it is my bread to know such." Umar cursed silently. Had the man no caution?

Kentar grinned. "That none can pay to tell. You may as well ask news of the most honored caliph's steps in his palace." He took a folded parchment from inside his thawb and offered it. "I pay you for this. The parchment needs to find my friend's friend across the sea. In Britannia, in Humber port, it is for a Lord Dain. He stays at a house called stronghold Cierheld, in the mountains. Here is the name and place written in his tongue." Kentar's eyes narrowed, and he half withdrew the bit of parchment. "Be sure you send a messenger with a straight tongue and sure hands, and you will receive as much as this again." He tossed the bag of coin in the air and then dropped it into Kaish's palm. "Bring Lord Dain's answer. My master is generous to faithful messengers."

Kaish hummed, content. "It shall be as you command."

Kentar turned away then glanced back. "My master has hopes that the furs in the mountains this year are good; there will be leather at least. He's a sharp one for trade, and he sniffs something of profit in the wind."

Then he was gone. Kaish concealed the parchment and coin about his person and pottered over his wares, laying out a scarlet rug, rolling up another of royal blue, lifting it to his shoulder.

This time Umar would not touch him, for he was angry enough to strangle him. He whispered in his ear, "Kaish," and slipped back as Kaish whirled, ducking the carpet that came for his head. Umar's dagger nestled at his side a moment after.

Kaish sniffed, glared at the blade, snarled, "You are an Efreet—not a man," and stalked inside. He lit a lamp and wet his lips with a scowl. "I listened for a Djinn in vain. It may be I need a talisman just for you." With a last dark look he took Kentar's parchment out of his sash and studied the letter's seal. He imprinted it in a bit of soft clay, and slipped his dagger tip expertly beneath the hardened wax. "There." Motioning to the table before him, he left the parchment open, his gaze avoiding it. "I see no words. May your eyes be swift. When it is resealed none will know. My messenger comes soon."

Umar grunted and read in the candle's wavering light.

My dear sister, we are well. Faisal shelters us in his tents. How are your father and your stronghold? Have you news of Hamal? The wazir presses close through Umar's Hand, though all in the desert mislead him.

I miss the Umar who threw my staff to me. He has changed. No one here dares give Tae away. They would die at their brothers' hands—or Tae's. At least such is his reputation. At the caliph's word, the Kathirib will attack to bring the Twilket and Aneza to the caliph's mind over a tax on goods brought through the sands.

I miss our sparring; I practice still. Here I sleep alone, without you at my back. I would I could be at yours. A scop is not needed here, nor a scribe, nor my staff.

Tae says not to be anxious, the Master of the Stars has all in hand. I know that, but I cannot feel it. The only thing to do is what he has laid before me.

Faisal has enemies among the sheyk's men. Their leader, one Hafiz, would be sheyk when Gershem is gone. And Gershem will not choose between them as yet. It threatens the Twilkets from within—and so the peace of the Oasis of Oaths. Faisal sees this; he is not dim.

Hafiz seeks to humble him before their warriors. I wish I could stand for him—the prince does not deserve their hard words. He shields us from the Kathirib, though he is angry at times and struck by dark moods.

I wish I knew how to protect with a touch, as you do, but Tae thinks it best not. When will our father see I am ready? When will I not need to be protected? Am I so different?

I must be strong. You know me, sister. You have my love. I am writing our Chronicle from the time that Ali Ben Aidon took us. If the Master of the Stars allows, you will read it.

Send Hamal swiftly. Umar hunts us. We have heard no mention of you in any news of the desert or of Baghdad. You are in our hearts.

The Master of the Stars keep you in his hand. Your sister by blood, by hearth and by salt. I must end, but you will be glad to know Cicero will have pups soon by Sahar, Faisal's hound. You could hunt every morn here, in the hills.

Your sister, Alaina Ilen.

His jaw knotted, Umar turned away and stepped out into the dark. He did not toss Kaish a coin. The rug seller kept his life.

Prince Faisal, the Twilket Wolf, sheltered in his tents one with the ability to enter any man's chamber at night and leave without stirring a curtain. A man who could kill with a blow; who once led the Aneza to victory, mayhap with the help of Djinn.

Umar's smile held no humor. He would gain the death touch for his master. His master said wait, watch. He would obey. Soon all would see the wisdom and strength of the wazir's Hand. Now for the hunt, the slow stalk and the pounce—to divide the weak from the strong.

§

Sahar lay at Faisal's feet in his grandfather's tent, her belly heavy with pups. Deep in dreams, Cicero curled around her and whuffled in her ear. She flicked it, licked her jaws, and heaved a great sigh. Faisal wanted to sigh as well. His back was cold.

Alaina knelt on the far side of the wide rug, her elbow on a pile of cushions, her head bent over her Chronicle. A bit of red-gold hair curled about her ear, beyond her kaffiyeh she had left down to keep the chill from her neck and the wind from her ears.

Though he gained strength every day, Sheyk Gershem had claimed the privilege of old bones and retreated behind the curtain to his bed. Tae snored lightly in the corner among a pile of cushions after a hard day of training with lances.

Faisal stretched his arms. He was a little sore himself, for he had sought to out-throw Tae. He had succeeded by a hair. Tae had a natural gift for striking a precise mark with any weapon. Faisal grinned. He was blessed Tae had not practiced lance-throwing a day more before his challenge. Hafiz had scored behind them both. His scowl had set his lesser place in stone in the minds of their Twilket brothers. Faisal's grin disappeared. Hafiz's ill-will at his loss gained him no voices around the night fires. He drummed his fingers on his knee, chin in hand.

Sahar had found a companion to run beside her. How long would it take for him to know Alaina's mind? She said little about what pleased her or did not, though when she thanked him it was heartfelt, as when a moment agone he brought the lamp for her. A step sounded without. Cicero and Sahar's heads rose.

Faisal straightened, and Alaina put down her quill. Tae's snore stopped.

Kentar slipped inside. He breathed heavily, and his green cloak sparkled with drizzle. He smelled of juniper and haste. Tae sat up and rubbed his neck. Faisal rose. "I will call for tea."

Kentar did not seem to see him, but dropped to his knees with a jerk beside Tae. "You must go with the first light—I have eyes on my back. We are betrayed. Kaish—" He coughed.

Tae stood, his face full of concern, and grasped Kentar's shoulders, guiding him to a seat on the cushions. Alaina laid aside her parchments and went out, for hot tea Faisal thought, and food, for Kentar's face was grey.

"Five sunrises I've come, with every wile. It may not suffice. I left the letter with Kaish to avoid my death." He looked up at Tae, pleading. "I had to live to bring you the news." He thrust a silvery bundle into Tae's hands, almost weeping. "For you and Sarni. The wazir's Hand follows his message, and you must not be here. You must not."

"I thank you for the warning, old friend." Tae unwrapped the bundle. Faisal stared at a hand of costly Persian pottery. The tips of the graceful fingers, a woman's hand severed at the wrist, were stained red with henna. The heat of dread spread in Faisal's stomach.

Tae cocked his head at Faisal thoughtfully. "Either he's after our blood, which we knew, and he means to flush us from cover, or . . ."

"Or he knows of Alaina and me," Faisal finished, "and this signifies he knows the ruse we plan. But how can that be? Even Sarni—" he caught himself. "Even Alaina does not know, none knew but we alone."

Gershem moved the inner curtain aside, staring at them, blinking.

"Sheyk Gershem." Tae bowed. "We thank you for your hospitality, but we will go now. First we will gather what we must. I will not bring death on your people." He glanced at Faisal, and Faisal nodded.

Gershem would send out lancers to circle the camp and riders to warn the far-flung tents. Twilkets would go out behind Tae and Alaina and confuse their tracks. He himself would shadow his guests. Faisal's heart beat heavy and fast. There would be no seeking Alaina's quill now, or her quick smile, only swift running.

When had she become more to him than any other face? A face that demanded what he could not give? She held more than a link to peace among the tribes, she was somehow more than a scribe with an unfortunate bent for trouble.

Sahar licked Kentar's face, while Cicero moved to Alaina's side. Faisal's fists clenched. There would be no warm touch for him. But if she lived, it would be enough. He swallowed. It must be.

She had enough enemies hunting her. It was time the Hand learned what it meant to have a wolf on their trail. Two wolves, and a pack of Twilkets. He looked at Tae, grim, and Tae said, "Bring another lance. We hunt together."

6

Wazir's Daughter

He heals the brokenhearted. ~ Psalms 147:3

First light pearled the sky. Faisal watched Alaina, who rested her hand on her mare's back, ready to depart. "Would you keep Cicero? I would not part him from Sahar." She looked up at Faisal, and down again. Her breath steamed in the cold. She leaned down to stroke Cicero and then urged him away from her knees.

Fasial was not fooled. He saw the tears in her eyes and gave her a small smile. "They will be well, my brother, until you return." Alaina blinked at him, gave him a short nod. He wanted to put his arm about her. Those who hunted her would find him a wolf indeed.

A yell rose outside camp on the desert side. Over the thudding of distant camel pads the sound of a single horse drew nearer.

Tae shouted, "Circle!" Farook dashed among the tents, yelling. Men poured out with swords and lances and bows, some running for their mounts, some toward Faisal.

"Lances!" Faisal bellowed. Warriors leapt to form a ring of seven lance tips around him and his guests. Others moved outward in an expanding ripple.

Around the edge of the tents a figure in billowing red and black thundered into sight, molded along the neck of a magnificent white horse. The rest could not be far behind. The hunters had come.

The white Arabian slowed as its rider guided its head around, and it shied to a stop on glorious haunches with a snort and a toss of its silver mane. In the wazir's red, the woman rode well. A veil covered her face in the manner of Oman. Sand fell from her high-flung hand in the sign of peace. Every warrior was caught in Faisal's silent hesitation.

Behind her, a camel ran hard ahead of five others. A young Arab bestrode it easily, lance ready, alert and lithe as a gazelle, eyes restless, watchful. A hunter. Behind him a smaller figure rode veiled and cloaked in a woman's brown *aba*. Four more men flanked, two carrying swords and two with a white knuckled grip on their daggers. Faisal's mouth tightened. Those four were no warriors, merely household slaves about a serving woman.

His gaze flicked back to the foremost rider. Why was a woman of the wazir's house here instead of Umar's Hand?

"On you be peace in the name of Allah," she called in a sweet voice. "I would see the scribe. I have a message from the wazir, the most excellent."

Faisal tensed when Tae motioned him forward. He stooped for a bit of earth and stepped through the circle of lancers. The dust fell from his hand in a curtain.

It was peace, for the moment. "Sarni!" He called over his shoulder, hoping she was near.

"I'm here," Alaina said behind him, her voice low.

"Ah. Tae says we will take the wazir's message."

"Yes," she said, and walked past him, unarmed. Why had she left her staff on her horse? Faisal scanned the junipers and tents and his men, who waited hawkish and ready as more Twilkets rode toward him with Hafiz at their head. Hafiz ordered, "To the sheyk!" and half the mounted warriors with him rode toward Gershem's tent, even as Alaina passed him, head high, every line of her crying scorn for the danger. Cicero walked at her side, Farook behind her shoulder.

Faisal stepped forward, but Tae shook his head and mounted smoothly, walking his horse out after Alaina. He halted and inclined his head to the young Arab, ignoring the wazir's messenger. Faisal held his breath. He could not mistake another hunter.

Alaina stopped a length from the woman in red, and also looked past her. "Zoltan," She said quietly, and nodded. The young Arab returned her greeting with the faintest smile.

Faisal drew a breath, nostrils flaring. He was torn as a wolf should never be, his purpose to protect both Alaina and his grandfather foiled by the wazir's messenger at a stroke.

At last Alaina turned to the woman, who had not moved a muscle despite the insult offered. Alaina's chin lifted. "I am Sarni. What message may I take from the wazir, blessed be he, to my illustrous master, Sheyk Gershem of the sands?"

The messenger bent her veiled head, a swaying fringe of black beads edging the red across her face. She hesitated, her soft voice on the edge of hearing. "My father has bid Umar and his Hand cease their hunt. The Kathirib will not come. Kyrin Cieri has fulfilled her task." The wazir's daughter straightened and cried over the head of the crowd, "The wazir accepts one named Tae Chisun and—the scribe with him. For they have come into his favor."

She dropped her veil below her eyes, and her voice rose. Her mount danced, uneasy. "The honored wazir is willing to overlook the matter of the unpaid taxes, if you will offer a small token of esteem. With thirty camels the most exalted caliph will account the Twilkets acquitted. If they cease to stir the hearts of his people and instead guard his trade-way with the same bright lances and fiery spirit with which they opposed him."

Faisal frowned as murmurs rose around him. "Why does this woman come? Thirty camels—does the wazir seek to shame us? He would have us guard the merchants . . . against whom? Is her tongue twisted? "

The sun was rising. Faisal flicked his hand sharply in Tae's gesture, and behind him his men grounded their lances with disgruntled thumps. He walked forward as the wazir's daughter slid from her saddle and leaned to whisper earnestly in Alaina's ear.

Faisal's eyes narrowed. There was no pack beast among the strangers, and the serving woman shook, gripping her saddle with pale fingers, as if she feared he would rip her from her seat and eat her. Uncertain as owls new-woken from a burrow, the two older men in household thawbs eyed him. All of them were afraid. Too afraid.

Umar and Kaish had read Kentar's letter five suns ago. Time enough for treachery. There was yet no bond of bread and salt.

Faisal positioned himself beside Alaina, ready to draw his blade, his jaw set. "What lie is spoken here?" He ignored Alaina's elbow in his side. "You are no emissary. Your people fear. What does the Hand of the wazir give for baiting his enemies?"

The woman in red loosed Alaina's sleeve and faced him, her head high. "I lie not."

"Why does the wazir send his daughter instead of his Hand?"

"I go where I am sent." Outlined by kohl, the hot fire in her gaze drove deep her cold words. "I am Hala, daughter of Sirius Abdasir, wazir to the caliph. I bear word to friends before they attack a Hand that is turned from them." Hala drew a folded parchment from beneath her aba, and her voice was a lowered lance. "From Kyrin Cieri, for him." Her chin indicated

Tae. Either Sirius wanted the missive unread by his Hand, he thought little of his blood, or he wound some other coil.

Tae strode forward and took the letter. He opened it with a whisper of parchment, and his gaze flicked down the page. At last he looked up. "These are Kyrin's words. The wazir's favor is returned to us."

Hala met Faisal's quiet stare, her lip curled, guarded. He gave her a prince's bow. All would become clear in time. It always did. "Then peace be to you and yours in the name of Sheyk Gershem Ben Salin. I am prince Faisal. You are well come to our tents." He hoped it was so.

Alaina glared at him. Did she catch the withdrawal in his voice, or merely disapprove his challenge in general? But he would not fail her for lack of caution.

"Yes, well come, daughter of my brother." Gershem strode toward them. His kaffiyeh glistened in the morning, his tan cloak gracing his best white thawb. "Come, be refreshed by the fire of Sheyk Gershem Ben Salin. We will speak of these thirty camels." His eyes held the keen light of a man eager for the thrust and parry of trade and bargains to advantage.

Hala bowed acceptance, and her companions dismounted.

Faisal gestured, and Farook rushed to take the reins of the newcomers' beasts. Hafiz and his men waited in a proud semicircle around their sheyk. Gershem held out his thin arm toward Hafiz's tent in a gesture of welcome, his smile broad.

Beside Gershem, Hala and her serving girl moved under the wide felt roof, Faisal followed with Tae and Alaina, and the warriors walked a few paces behind. Hafiz closed in last. The rest of the Twilket men would join them when all was secure in camp, the women and children calmed, and the sentries doubled.

Every blade had two edges. Faisal grimaced. He should have ordered Hafiz to see to his grandfather himself, then Hafiz's actions would have strengthened his cause, not displayed his prince as a lackwit. If Hafiz's heart had been his, not ordering him would have been a sign of his prince's trust. But as it was . . .

Zoltan walked beside Cicero. The hunter stroked the saluki's head. Cicero panted happily, his breath white in the morning chill, and licked his hand. The young Arab caught Faisal's eye, held it, and smiled.

Faisal's mouth curved though his face felt wooden. It seemed everyone except him had a part in Alaina and her affairs. How did Tae and Alaina know Zoltan? His feet, hands, and face showed signs of desert sun yet his hair remained dark, without the tawny sun's kiss that marked the desert born. His eyes roved over the people, the tents, the hills and flats around them, wary. Had he been a friend to Alaina?

Faisal's mouth twisted as if on a sour fig. And the others? *Did* this Hala speak with the wazir's voice? He would tread warily before the snake's den.

In Gershem's tent they settled across from each other in loose groups, cross-legged on the rug among richly embroidered cushions. Hafiz's slave was ready with honeyed cardamom tea. That one was a good match for Hafiz, who seized every opportunity to use the letter of hospitality to rip out its spirit. It should be his grandfather's slave who so cheerfully took the small cups to his guests on the rug, in his own tent. The sheyk's wife should watch from behind the curtain, not Hafiz's Basimah, whispering with her women of preparations for the guesting platter.

He must let the insult go. There was more at stake. Faisal let out a long quiet breath and glanced at Alaina. Seated beside him and Tae—her kaffiyeh in a quick-wound turban, her legs crossed—she in no way revealed she was a woman. Her hands were quiet on her knees. His belly clenched again.

Hafiz must not know what she was, not until his grandfather formally approved his and Tae's plan, and could hold the approval of the elders. But if the Kathirib did not ride to raid there would be less pressing need to forge strong ties between his people and the Aneza. His brow furrowed. Was the caliph so weak, to give up his prey so easily? Or was it the power of his wazir that lay concealed behind both the caliph's tax and his forgiveness?

Sheyk Gershem inquired into the wazir's health and that of Hala and her companions, then turned to Hala's news. "How is it that *you* come to us as a token of trust, O most precious of the wazir, instead of the most honorable wazir's Hand himself?"

Straight to the attack. Gershem was not weak. He had not missed Hala's avoidance of a prince's question. Faisal smiled to himself, even as the scent of roasting goat and spiced rice for the coming feast tickled his nose. Every murmur ceased, every eye on the wazir's daughter.

Hala paused. Her indrawn breath pulled at her veil. She said softly, "I have sworn the sister bond to Kyrin Cieri. Of bread and salt and blood—for she saved me from worse than the Kathirib." Beside him, Alaina's grip whitened on her knees. Hala continued, "Our houses are now bound. And through the house of Cieri, now bound to you, to both honorable Aneza and Twilket." She smiled, and looked to the tea cradled in her lap. A few stared then shrugged, while the women serving about the tent buzzed in amazement.

Faisal said nothing. That seemed truth, one of the reasons the price of enmity might be revoked. But *Kyrin* saved the wazir's daughter? There had been no time for Kyrin to save anyone during her flight across the desert to Sirius's ship, the *Sabra*. If it were so, Tae would have told him. She had gone to seek Hamal. Faisal sat back and fingered his chin. Was Hala perhaps Hamal?

The sister oath was binding—if Sirius Abdasir approved his daughter's word. But she challenged them all, and something remained untold. Hafiz bore a thunderous scowl. Because he wished time to cast dirt on Kyrin's name, or did he think Hala's words also a ruse? Faisal watched Hafiz narrowly. *He* would have thought so, except for Tae's witness to the letter.

Alaina held that missive in her hand. She read the parchment, folded it, and opened it again, smoothing it on her knee as if she could reach Kyrin through it.

Tae watched Hala, who spoke now in the way of a guest in courteous nothings to Gershem. Tae's creased face and slanted almond eyes gave nothing to any watcher. Faisal schooled his own.

Cicero lay against Alaina's back, Sahar curled up against both, snoring. Alaina had one hand on Cicero's knobby backbone, doubtless glad not to be parted from him. He raised his slim, noble head as Hala spoke, seeming to catch the excitement in the air. At least the cushions were softer than hooves pounding under them in flight day after day, from Umar and his Hand.

During a pause, Hala reached aside to her serving girl, took a bundle from her brown lap, and rose. She faced Alaina. "Jachin of my house asked me to give this to one who could take it to Kyrin of Cieri." Hala walked across the rug and laid the gift in Alaina's lap. Faisal forced down his anger as she approached. Why did Hala not send one of her servants with the gift, in the proper way? The men of her household watched with dull eyes, as if they would rather be elsewhere. Except for the young Arab. Something was not right.

Alaina stiffened when she touched the bundle, but bowed over her knees. "I thank you. Bid Jachin be well, and peace to him." She said nothing else, though Hala waited a moment.

Then Faisal did glare. Across from him the Arab stiffened, and Faisal glanced at him in warning.

Hala's back straightened, and she stalked back to her place. The girl in brown whispered hurriedly in her ear, blushing every time her glance crossed Faisal's. Faisal looked away. The wazir's messenger brought more curses than blessings.

Gershem smiled and clapped his hands. "We have been honored. Forty camels, not thirty, will return with you from our tents, Hala of the house of Abdasir. It will not be said that Gershem Ben Salin of the Twilkets is less than generous when his heart and those of his brothers are glad for peace."

"Hear, hear!" Faisal lifted his voice among others. Negotiation for peace was begun. It was not yet sealed.

Gershem said kindly, "The wife of our worthy Hafiz has prepared you a tent, Hala of the house of Abdasir. Would you be pleased to go and rest then return to break your fast at my fire?"

Hala kept her eyes on the blue-and-green patterned rug. "You are indeed most generous and wise, a great sheyk. My heart warms under your roof with promise of peace." She and her serving girl rose and followed Basimah out.

Faisal stared after the wazir's daughter and her servants thoughtfully. "What do you say, Sarni? Is there deep water here?"

"Oh yes." Alaina eyed their backs. "Though one who carries a message may be but a mouth, ignorant of the heart that beats behind it."

Despite her generous words her face was pale granite, her green eyes molten with flecks of gold. She clutched the gift for Kyrin to her. Faisal cocked a brow but said nothing.

His Twilket brothers were gathered thick around the rug, while latecomers clustered outside the tent. Some rejoiced already, while others watched, waiting on their sheyk's word.

Hafiz picked his way past the men gathered at the door and settled near Gershem, who sipped his tea, his shoulders beginning
to sag. As Hafiz stepped between Faisal and his grandfather,
Cicero growled low in his throat. Alaina smiled, with a twist of
her lips, and fingered his ears. "Yes, noble one, I know, but we
must not *say* his step reeks of jackals and carrion." Faisal choked
on a laugh. With a bright-eyed glance at him, Alaina murmured,
"I once thought the prince his kin."

Faisal fought the twitch of his mouth. He touched Alaina's
knee. "I will see what this *jackal* speaks in our sheyk's ear."

Alaina sniffed and her gaze, Sarni's gaze, held clear-eyed
challenge. "May not all know?" With a courteous clearing of
her throat to gather the attention of the men, she turned to
Gershem. "Wise Sheyk, your tent has sheltered me, your meat
has strengthened me, your wisdom and peace have healed my
heart. Your noble warrior"—she nodded to Hafiz—"has asked
your counsel. What does he say? What will the warriors of the
Twilkets do?"

Hafiz shot her an irritated glare. "I but ask if this *woman,* who
claims to speak for the wazir and rides in the place of a man, is
indeed his mouth."

"I, Sarni, am not so learned. Yet what besides an oath of blood
could drive so precious a jewel from her father's house to warn a
friend, and even friends of a friend? And there is the message."
Alaina held it up. "Need calls forth many qualities, in women
of a high house as much as among the lords of the desert. And
this Hala of Abdasir's house trusts your wisdom"—she looked
around at them—"wisdom as of the lions of the desert, who will
test her words and see where the Kathirib camp lies. Judge not
the wazir so foolish as to sacrifice his only camel to his enemy."

Hafiz's face soured. Gershem's mouth crinkled in a smile. The sheyk's hand shook around his bronze cup, the surface of the tea shivering. The goat could not roast too quickly for him.

Faisal stood in the laden silence. "A just question, Sarni. When it is answered and the wazir's word proves true, let us hunt again the raiders who plague our incense route. Let us gather the spices and the gold—and add righteous peace to our tents."

Murmurs of agreement among the warriors upheld him. Faisal raised his arm. "Is our sheyk not wise as the fox, swift as the falcon, and deserving of his seat? His hand has not faltered in this. It will not falter. I give you Gershem Ben Salin!"

"Sheyk! Sheyk Gershem, blessed of Allah!"

Hafiz's glare would be a blade in his heart if it had substance. Faisal turned from him as Kentar stepped inside the tent and bowed toward Gershem. "Ah salan alaykum."

"Ahlan, Kentar!" A chorus of welcome greeted him.

Faisal inclined his head and sank down on his cushion; he had said enough. What timely news did Kentar bring?

The dalil settled himself with Tae and Gershem and looked to his sheyk as he set his hand on Tae's shoulder with a wrinkled grin. "My sheyk, it is done. Our riders will return by the last light. Then we will know."

Faisal did not let his surprise touch his face. Tae had already sent men out to find the Kathirib. Or did Kentar speak of the Hand?

The sheyk said, "A straight tongue is well for the peace. We will be ready for peace, and ready for war. We must tread this ground with care."

Indeed. The Hand of the wazir was not to be trusted without a watch upon him. The prince's questions were endless, the answers elusive. Perhaps Gershem tested them all? Did Hafiz mean yet deeper mischief? And did Hala know the wazir wished a deadly knowledge from Tae and Alaina, or was she but a pawn?

§

"Nimah." Hala ran her hand over the soft bed rug, drawn up to her chin. "Did they not treat me as the wazir's daughter and listen to my words? It has gone well, I think, do you not?"

"Yes, mistress." Nimah rolled over, the beginnings of a smile on her face—then her eyes widened and she flung back her rugs, scrambling for her feet.

Tent cloth rustled behind Hala.

She rolled over swiftly, but her legs tangled with the rug, and she reached for a heavy pottery lamp behind her shoulder. The heavy felt wall dropped back into place, silhouetting a figure in a dark thawb and kaffiyeh, rising in the light.

"Be gone!" Hala raised the lamp. "You dare come here in violation of the sheyk's guests—" A small hand on her arm stopped her.

"Alaina," Nimah breathed, and ran to her.

Hala set down the lamp and crossed her arms to conceal her shaking hands. The Arab youth embracing Nimah was indeed Sarni—or Alaina—the sister Kyrin told her of. Though Alaina greeted her with few words in the sheyk's tent. It was not the kindness she had heard of, though mayhap Sarni's tongue was sharp because she feared others' knowledge of her secret?

Nimah chattered like a parrot, bouncing on her toes. "I showed the exalted wazir the fruit of my needle, Alaina, and I am now the first keeper of his robes. I also serve my mistress." She held out her hand toward Hala, her face glowing. "My mistress brings news of Kyrin—" Alaina murmured in her ear. "It will be as you wish," Nimah said, and passed in front of Hala to kneel on her rug. She looked from one to the other in delight and expectancy.

Alaina stared at Hala without speaking.

Hala blinked. If only her heart did not yet thump with fear—fear seared into her soul by those men who had come to her so many times before—when she was bound. But there was no way Alaina could know of that. Hala gestured to the rugs in gracious invitation, glad she wore her red thawb with the flowing sleeves, hemmed with bands of black. The colors of her father lent her the authority she did not feel.

"Do sit, sit with us!" Nimah patted the tent rug, aglow with excitement.

"I am well enough."

A small frown crossed Nimah's face. "But this is Hala, the one Kyrin—"

"I know." Alaina smiled gently at Nimah.

Hala's face flushed. Why did she refuse to speak to her?

"I must know if Umar hunts us. Burn it, is Jachin truly free? And what of Nara?"

"But—" Nimah glanced aside at Hala and continued in a rush, "Hala will tell you—"

"I will not disturb your mistress's rest more than I have."

Hala stared at Alaina, and her mouth hardened into a line. Alaina's small smile seemed to say she was not displeased at her fright. She had not missed her grip on the lamp.

Nimah's face fell. She bit her lip, and Hala laid her hand on her arm. "You do not disturb, Alaina. I walked with Kyrin of Cieri in her land, and I know—"

Alaina growled, "You know nothing! You could never know her as I, who have gone through fire and blood and death with her."

Enough blind ignorance was enough. Hala leaned forward, quivering. "I *was* dead—and she returned me to life. The men of your land are lower than accursed dogs. Some of the men here are no better! I would sink my cousin's falcon blade in their hearts if I had her strength! I would not hide behind words!"

Alaina stepped closer. "Falcon blade? Dogs? *You* speak of blades and dare talk of my hiding?" Her glance went meaningfully to the lamp in Hala's hand. "Many men are dogs, of whatever land, and women, too. Hah! You don't even carry a blade, and you have not the arms for it. No dagger in *your* hand could pierce a close-woven thawb. Mere threads would turn the blow! And words—sometimes words are the only things that can bring justice, turn aside ugliness, or bring beauty home to a heart!"

Hot words heated Hala's throat, forced themselves out. "The falcon of my house can cut through any heart!"

Alaina's mouth tightened. "Kyrin's falcon dagger?"

"It is sharp." Hala glared at her.

Alaina sighed, her shoulders drooping. "It could." She looked up. "Does Umar yet hunt us?"

Hala swallowed. Nimah touched her hand. "Mistress, Umar, the Hand I mean, was in your father's presence. When you told the wazir, blessed be he, how Kyrin took you from your chains, I saw Umar turn pale as goat cheese with wrath. Then, he reddened as a pomegranate when the most excellent charged him to guard you when you walk out of your courts. He is not a kind man. Less so when he found his reward taken by your sudden return, mistress."

Hala stood straighter. "He will guard me as my father commands and find greater repayment."

"Then why is he not here?" Alaina asked.

"This time it was better so." She could not show weakness. She need not say she had come at great cost to keep her oath to a friend, and to win her father's smile again.

Nimah's forehead wrinkled. "But the wazir, when he called me to serve you, his face was as iron. Surely he has not held—"

Hala shook her head against the shortness of her breath. "His anger is not against you, but it is hot. My father yet searches for Hamal, or news of him, though he sent Kyrin for me." All hope had gone with Hamal after so long a count of years. Hamal, who would have given her father her bride-price, even now, after what she would not give had been forced from her by men.

Hala swallowed memories of pain. Heat burned her cheeks, and she glared at Alaina. "My father is angry that I can no longer wed. I have borne much, even your sister's letter to you, with word of peace and goodwill, and you have nothing for me but an asp's bitterness? If you think evil of me, kill me yourself." It would stop the pain. Did her father even love her? She did not think he would smile at her again.

"It shall not be!" Nimah grabbed her hand and Alaina's, kneeling between them. "Kyrin—she holds my heart also. Do not dishonor her." Her voice broke. "Or yourselves. You are my sun and moon."

Hala let out a breath through her nose. "No. It was but a passing thought." Nimah was right, no matter how much pain roiled through her.

Alaina said in a small voice, her head turned away, "Forgive me, Hala."

Hala reached for her hand. It was cold and damp as tears long shed. That bowed head, so alone. Did she to, feel powerless? She herself had been lost, when Kyrin reached out to her. Hala said hoarsely, "I take no offense. You miss your sister? She is worth missing."

Alaina wiped her nose, and choked, "Yes, Kyrin is worth—missing."

Hala remembered a willowy figure with dark eyes and hair who offered the sister-bond—to a broken, angry spirit in despair. That gift taken, the haft of the falcon dagger in Kyrin's hand had shifted. The Damascus blade gleamed with sudden promise of better things than death. In Allah's kingdom there was nowhere to cast her burden. nothing to wipe out her stains. The stains of her guilt, regardless of her captors evils.

Kyrin swore she had found life with the Master of all, that all her evil was cleansed. Though she had past wounds enough, they were healing. Hala gulped. The falcon's amber eyes had glistened with her sorrow. With sorrow for her cousin, and for her dead hope of a husband and children. The falcon's deep gaze— like Kyrin, the falcon never gave up. Neither did their Master. The bright edge of the falcon called her to joy, to strength beyond herself. She must speak.

Desperately, she turned and wrapped her arms around Alaina and Nimah. Doing nothing led to death. Death of the soul and death of the mind. Death she knew too well. "Alaina? Who—who is this Master your sister speaks of? She says he is—a Father."

Alaina gaped. "Yes. He is also—God. His pure blood washed away our evils. If we take his gift. Then we are his."

"Let him take me." In the safety of her sisters' encircling arms, Hala began to sob. She would live and face her father. Her foray into the desert would forge peace between Baghdad and the tribes, peace without bloodshed. It would strengthen the caliph's rule. No one would speak of her ride—but the peace would remain. Though she retired behind the women's curtain to enjoy almond cakes, poetry, and the raising of others' children, when the need arose she would have that, though she kept herself veiled before men.

Her sisters hugged her, and healing was a new shape in Hala's mind, cast from a forge of pain. A moment of fresh life, however dim and hard to make out. She would seek it. She had a Father.

7

Heart and Word

Love bears all things... endures all things. ~ 1 Corinthians 13:7

Alaina woke. After a night begun in anger and sorrow that ended in laughter and warm arms, she had stumbled wearily to bed a bare watch before the dawn wind tugged at her flailing tent flap. It touched her face with chill fingers. The door should not be open. Her skin prickled.

She half expected to hear Cicero's bark and the snarling, closing cry of Umar's Hand in answer. But Umar hunted them no longer. Parchment lifted and sank behind her, the pages whispering. She turned. Her Chronicle, the stack of parchments on the shelf—it should be too heavy for the wind to move.

She rose and grabbed the few lonely pages that were left, her heart beating in her throat. Who would steal Kyrin's Chronicle or her other scribbles? Alaina's mouth flattened. Was Hafiz that desperate for more words to throw at Faisal? Hah! She would give him words, though not to his taste. And to come into her tent? The coward. Could he sink any lower?

Alaina yanked up her hair with furious fingers, pulled her kaffiyeh around her face then changed her mind and tucked it all up into a turban. The cloth framing her features made her appear womanly. She could not afford to be thought so, not now.

Had Hafiz taken her things while she was with Hala, or while she slept? The jackal. Worse, did he send another to do it for him? Hands clenched, she strode out of the tent. She would be sleeping with Cicero at her feet from now on.

The tents she stalked past were almost deserted, but she came upon a crowd of women and children about the fringes of a circle of men gathered before Gershem's tent. Alaina hesitated, and rose on her toes to see over their heads.

In a clear space in the midst of the people, Faisal and Hafiz stood before the sheyk's door, the prince's every fiber taut with furious fire, the sheyk's first warrior cold as stone, his eyes unmoving.

Not again. Burn the man. Alaina brushed past robed shoulders. She would make Hafiz acknowledge her right to speak. What did he charge the prince with now, neglect of his sheyk when Hala threatened the camp? And where was Farook? He was never far from Faisal's side, but she had not seen him since the beginning of the feast. Surely Hafiz did not use her words against the prince again.

Before she reached them, the first warrior's mouth parted in a grin. His deep, certain voice slipped about the silent warriors with their curved daggers at their waists, the sun-kissed heads of their wives and children around them. "Do you say these are not your words, my prince?" He held a piece of parchment up before Faisal's face.

"What does it mean when Hala Abdasir, daughter of the wazir, departs so soon after her welcome feast, and this is found? Is she false? Are *you?*" He shook the parchment under Faisal's nose, his glare sweeping those around him. "Listen, my brothers, to his word to you." Hafiz straightened, solemn, and lifted his voice. "'I cannot abandon my people—though the mountains and the desert do not seek my blood as some of them do, with malice. I will see the jackals among us, who wish sheep for their jaws, crushed. Power gives no man the right to challenge another. The Master of the Stars' command gives me the right, since he has placed me here. All who seek me will find a wolf.'"

Hafiz paused, his nostrils pinched. "I think this 'Master of the Stars' command' refers to this God of yours." He pointed a finger at Faisal. "Who gives you the right to rule without your brothers' yea or nay? Who do you name jackal, my brother? I— or any other who finds it fit to lead our people?"

Pale and tense, Faisal said nothing. Alaina raised her hand to her mouth then forced it down, shaking. Her scribing had given a flow to Faisal's words to her—they were not his alone. Hafiz had left out the bit about a leader's responsibility to act righteously. He would.

"And as for our malice, what is in *your* heart? Are you a wolf to our enemies, or perhaps to us? Do you use the Kathirib threat to gain power among us during our need, power sealed by the deadly hand of your trained assassin?"

Alaina wormed through the last circle of warriors on a hot wave of anger. Her voice cut across Hafiz's.

"What of those who steal another's words, words not meant for them? What of one who twists words as he wishes? What of parchments *twice* stolen from a scribe? What of that, noble Hafiz?" She held out her hand. "Those are *my* words you hold. Give them back." Give him little explanation, and fewer things to wrest from their true meaning, though the damage was done.

Hafiz smiled again, slow and wide. Her stomach sank. *Burn me.*

"Ah, you demand, so like a woman. A woman—or should I say—a wife? The hidden wife of Tae Chisun, who yet bears Twilket blood on his hands."

Alaina drew herself up. "In time of war he killed a man who came for his life in the dark, attacking his back!" The women and warriors around her murmured. If Hafiz truly wanted an enemy, well. "There is no fault you can lay on Tae Chisun's head. As for his wife—I am his daughter, though not by blood. Your heart is bitter for the death of your father's brother, but judgment of this matter was decided by your elders. Does their judgment not stand?"

Basimah gasped, and the women put their heads together. Some of the men frowned. Faisal looked from Hafiz to her, a line of uncertainty between his brows.

Hafiz's gaze intensified. "Who can tell how far your falseness goes? I do not judge our elders' decree, but your split tongue. Tell me, will poison find my tent, or an arrow or a stray blade take me on the hunt, or do you have the touch of death in *your* hands?"

Alaina gulped, with a catch of breath. He knew of the death touch. Faisal moved as if to speak, but Alaina lifted her chin, pushing down the upheaval inside. "I am not strong enough to kill with one blow. All in these tents know how I have served them with my staff, my quill, and my herbs."

Hafiz shook his head, his indignation melting into pity. "Ah, Sarni—but I do not know your true name. It matters not." He spread his arms in helplessness. "These parchments were under a stone at my fireside when my wife stirred the embers this light. Not many of us have the gift of the scribe."

You mean none other but I and the prince. Alaina swallowed.

"These must be our prince's words, for this scribe speaks of himself as a wolf, and who among us does not know he alone is called so? How can a Twilket prince turn so against his brothers?" He was asking her.

That was the bone he had wanted, and she had given it to him.

Faisal swallowed and dropped his gaze. Alaina's throat ached. *Oh Faisal, how could it come to this? I did not mean . . .*

Faisal looked up at her in hot misery, his hand resting on his blade, his shoulders taut. He growled, "Sarni, you—" Then spun back to Hafiz and opened his mouth. He stopped.

Tae stood before Gershem's tent flap as if he had grown there, Gershem at his shoulder. The sheyk's white head was high. His dark eyes snapped. He indicated Hafiz and said something in Tae's ear.

Tae's dark face was still. When he had gathered every eye he strode forward. He faced them all, loose and easy, hands at his sides. His voice rose mildly. "As for those words being your prince's, I know not. This I know. Alaina, whom you call Sarni, is my daughter in all but name. That marriage has been dissolved, as is your custom. Of this, your sheyk knows."

Heads turned. Gershem said, "It is so, I witnessed it."

Tae stared straight at Hafiz. "First warrior, I will overlook your stirring of blood that has been paid. The Nur-ed-Dam between us is dead." He paused.

A sigh ran through the crowd.

Alaina stirred. *Dead, until he has one of us in his hand. "Burn us" does not begin to cover it.*

Tae stepped to her side, his hand on her shoulder. "My daughter's tongue is straight. I ordered her deception for our lives—and for yours, that the Hand of the wazir might not fall on you. Now that warding is not needed. We are blessed with peace." Tae smiled. "Your prince, whom you accuse of hunting power, will seal that peace, with both the Aneza and the caliph. For your prince has asked my daughter's bride-price."

Alaina's mouth dropped open.

Tae laughed, suddenly light and free. He lifted his hands. "Who has ever seen our prince hunt anything with all his heart but a good horse, or a beast with horns and hooves for the pot, or a quiet day in the mountains?" He rubbed his chin meditatively. "I do grant you, in the matter of Alaina's bride-price he has been most persistent." Humor crooked his mouth. A low, appreciative laugh bubbled from many throats.

Hafiz looked from Tae to Faisal to her, and back at Gershem's satisfied face. His gaze swung to Alaina, black as poison. "Do not think to steal what is mine."

Her, steal from *him?* If he alluded to her bearing an heir for the prince, that was a small thing, distant from her. She felt a humming as of bees inside—and then flame burned them to ash. Something else loomed large. *Marriage.*

Tae had known of this. Even Gershem, his smile approving. And she with never a whisper. How could they?

Was this marriage a ruse they devised after Hala arrived, to solidify the Twilkets' position with the caliph? She glanced at Faisal, her breath coming hard. No. A smile twitched the corners of his mouth. He *dared* smile at her. No, it had been long-standing. He seemed rather pleased with himself, the jackal.

And Hafiz said Hala had gone, gone without a word to her this morn, Nimah and Zoltan also. Doubtless that was Tae or Faisal's doing—for some obscure good reason. She was holding her breath, there was no time to think, and she was going to cry. She stepped away from them.

Hafiz's scowl blackened his voice, overthick with respect. "My prince, you say you do not seek to lead our people. Tell me, how can that be if these are your words?" He shook the parchment.

In one stride Faisal was the width of a sword's blade from Hafiz. "I seek my people's well-being, as I have always done."

"Hafiz, my son," Gershem lifted his hands, "after they are wed they will go from here. Have you not seen how Faisal's heart wanders our land? It is not his path to stay among our tents.

Though he may return when he has blunted his lance against enough rocks and rain, our enemies and long hunts, when his bones ache as mine."

Gershem's voice sharpened, and he eyed them every one. "I have yet the strength to crush a wolf if it turns on my tents—as well as jackals. When I pass, my place will go to the one who best fits it. Our elders are not bereft of wisdom." His beard bristled, and the older heads among the warriors nodded, old backs straightening in pride.

Alaina closed her eyes. She could not be a weapon of warding. She could not bind the Twilket and Aneza tribes in the caliph's peace, however much Faisal loved his people. And Gershem did not promise his place would go to Hafiz.

But what did the sheyk mean, Faisal might return after blunting his lance against rain? That was curious. There was not much rain in the desert. Did he mean to go to the coastlands, or the mountains? She swallowed. The mountains, close to the coast, were beautiful. But wherever he went, it would not be with her. A man who barely spoke to her could not love her. He a prince, and she a peasant, not even of his desert. But she must not show her displeasure to all.

"Let the henna celebration be long!" Tae's hand descended on Alaina's shoulder. She started.

Faisal moved to face her, entirely too quickly. Tae set her hand in his.

For once Alaina agreed with Hafiz. Faisal did not love her, could not, she was not fit for him. He wanted only to protect his people. Was it not so? Her breath came fast.

Faisal's palm was dry and warm and his fingers closed about hers. A wolf's strength; he had that. Stay in this land always, without garden or court or poet—and never see Kyrin again?

Alaina swallowed hard, jerked her hand free, and backed up. *Burn it. Did they not have common courtesy?* "I, this—I did not know. I cannot—I must go." She turned blindly and ran.

In the scribe's tent she bent over the table, her face in her hands, tears wetting her fingers, her chest hot and tight. For Faisal to never speak a word, it was too cold, heartless. He could not love her. If only she might be with Kyrin in the forests of Britannia. Better a scop at Kyrin's side than lady of a desert. And worse than lady of a desert, even the mountains, to be keeper of a man who did not care for her. . . . how could she face anyone outside?

A light step pulled Alaina's head up and she scrambled to her feet. Faisal loomed against the light. Why had she come here, of all places? She shrank from him.

"Do you know what you have done?" His flat, emotionless words made her shiver more than if he'd cursed her.

"I've done nothing—" Her voice was small.

"Nothing but shame us and those who thought to secure our future." His anger dwindled to sadness as he looked at her.

"Did Tae say he sought my future?" It was half angry. *The time is right—be his friend.* Alaina sank back, staring at her hands. Tae had hinted at it. And said she would be protected. She was a fool and blind.

"Yes." Faisal sighed abruptly and sat at the end of the table. "You could have smiled and waited to speak to me. I would have listened. We thought you would understand the need: yours, mine, our people's."

"Why do you—need me?" She did not quite dare say 'want.' He could not mean that.

He stared at her, and that wolfishness of intent was back. "For my people, for your safety, and for myself. You are more than worthy. But now Hafiz—"

She could imagine Hafiz's wrath at Faisal's heightened position among his people as a bridge between Twilket and Aneza, the wazir and the caliph. And whenever Faisal left his people, her own higher place, associated as she was with Kyrin and Hafiz's long-held Nur-ed-Dam. All those things must be gravel to the first warrior's teeth. Besides the fact he was publicly set down a step.

"He laughs, and says it is my way of running from the lance," said Faisal bitterly.

That was far worse, for a prince. And she had given his enemy more than enough arrows to cast at him. Alaina covered her eyes. "I would not have him gloat. Forgive me." If she could only undo them.

"I do forgive. It was sudden news, and you have had much to bear." His gentle voice tightened. "But will you explain this?" Alaina looked up and took the parchment from his fingers, forcing herself not to step back as he rose carefully and came close. His hand was not quite steady, nor was hers. His eyes were dark, nostrils pinched, his mouth pressed white.

She read aloud slowly, "His Master of the Stars rules indeed, and teaches men to rule their passions, to grow—a most hard task." Beside it she'd written, "A flower growing in the desert. One who rules himself is fit to rule others." She had not meant to hurt him with the truth. She cupped her hand around the rumpled missive as if it were a lark that might fly from her. Anger surged in her, sudden and glorious. Fear fled, all veils ripped away. *Burn it*—no, she would leave those words behind and tell him. She said low, "Faisal, a fit word may work as a weapon or a shield, an apple of gold in a picture of silver—"

"Or in this, neither." He glared at her. "Nothing but to give laughter to fools!"

Alaina could not fend off his heat. She did not wish to. She stared into the shadows, choosing words. "I fight the evil I see, only not as Kyrin—"

"I do not speak of her—"

"Neither do I! Will you open your ears?" It was hard to think her way toward what formed in her mind.

He shut his mouth, a hard line.

Alaina rubbed her face wearily. *I fight with what has been given me, with what is given me in the moment.* "You asked me to write for you, once. But *your* words echoed inside me, and I wrote them in verse. Forget Hafiz! This, this is beautiful." She leveled the parchment at his chest. *"You* have the poetry of the desert in you." She stepped closer, almost touching him, and lifted her face, fierce. "Yes, I wrote this. You have a true heart, not of stone, though you love me not, burn it!" She shook. The words had slipped out, and the last were too much a part of her.

"You have a falcon's eyes, to see inside me?" It was low with threat.

Alaina winced but did not retreat. A falcon's eyes, he said, not blind fool. A falcon, and Kyrin. Kyrin. Had Kaish sent her letter on to her sister, or had he kept it for reasons of his own? But she must not grow suspicious of all men.

Enough. Her sister was far away. Faisal hung in the balance, his heart and spirit. Her words had hurt him. Could she stay now—for him? Or maybe for herself, even Tae. Had he sent Faisal after her?

She did not know. One thing she did know. The prince had been wounded, though she had not meant it. She must guard the truth *and* guard him from the harm she had brought. Hardship in life, given edge by the cruel inner voice, by the laughter of men—those could beat a soul into the ground. "A falcon's eyes, you say?" She glared at him. "I see you do not hunger for blood, as Hafiz does!" *Or Umar.*

"Do I not?" He cocked his head and his mouth parted in a thin smile, wolfish to the core.

"You—you ought to find someone who sees farther than your-self, if you are so blind!" She drew a deep breath. Was he angry with her, or Hafiz, or himself? "You *are* fit to lead, and ought not to turn aside from it."

"But by my own grandfather, I am sworn to leave." Faisal's brows snapped together. "The worst of it is, I cannot deny my words you wrote are true."

"So become what you have said, hold it fast! Let the jackal who hunts sheep find the wolf. Do not let Hafiz twist your words, or you. Whether you lead your Twilket brothers as sheyk or no."

"As you say, I have no wish to deny the truth." He smiled then, with all his heart in it. It was the sun after storm. "You have a way of making me see things."

Alaina felt herself shaken inside, and scowled.

He sobered. "And you, take truth to yourself, also."

"I?"

"Yes. Why do you say you cannot accept me? Why are you unsure?" Pain laced his voice and he looked down. "Kyrin spoke truer than she knew, seasons ago. We were too strong for each other, and on separate paths, she seeking her eyrie with the Master of the Stars, I flying beneath, through the dust of the deepest hell."

He looked up, earnest. "Now I go to the same eyrie, and I see you soaring beside me, over the green grass and cool water, with peace in your spirit. We could fly together." He touched her arm, then dropped his hand. "Each defending the other, we can defeat these gossip-mongers. No matter, that you do not possess the death touch. That is a small thing." He was laughing at her. Gently. "You are fierce enough without it."

He bent near, full of heat again. "Alaina, you need to be strong in *your* strengths, the gifts given *you*, not in another's. Not in Kyrin's—but Alaina's strengths—gifts from the Master of all. Take his truth to you; take joy in it. You are strong, Alaina. Know it."

She shivered. Her battle to accept her weaknesses, her struggle to find her place in the world, to be strong—he saw it? *Burn him—no, no.* But he did see too much.

The place she sought was not completely shaped, nor completely known. She wet her lips. "You could live with one who is a pawn of peace, not born of your sands, whom no other would have? You would have the—the heart of one who is spoiled?"

"Do not call yourself so! I have Tae's word you are not touched. Even if you had been, it would not be to your blame. That rests on Ali Ben Aidon's head."

Alaina's face burned. She was a healer; she should not blush at such things. She smoothed the paper in her hand.

His voice lowered. "I see your power. I would live with one who speaks truth, though it does not favor her. With one who picks battles that need fought, no matter how many lances oppose her—"

"Battles ill fought, this morn," she said. "Right words at an ill moment and ill words at the right moment."

"You do not start a battle with *me* that you cannot win." He was laughing at her again.

"Unless I must." A smile tugged at her mouth. He meant what he said.

"Yes." He stepped closer and whispered, "May no battle ever separate us long." His mouth came down on hers.

Thought fled in a warding fire of strength and understanding. The promise in his touch warmed her differently than any fire ever had. Could it be true . . .? She thought it was, and reached for him.

His hand folded around hers and he pulled back, leaving something hard and angular within her fingers. She held a brooch of black amber: a falcon, with eyes, beak, and wings detailed in silver.

Widespread wings. Kyrin's falcon brooch . . . no, did she not take hers with her? Alaina bit her lip. She had said she did not love falcons. She was not Kyrin. Or did Faisal simply give it for his own love of the bird, its power and skill and beauty?

His arms closed around her, folding her hands to her chest, and his whisper was warm in her ear. "Keep it. It will not bite. It is precious to me, as you are."

And so he holds my heart. After a long moment Alaina pulled away. Her blood raced with her breath.

It felt so good to be loved, and wanted, and to rest against him. She felt alive to the ends of her fingers. Yet—true safekeeping rested with no man, but with the Master of the Stars, who kept them all. And did she believe she could be a bridge? If only her heart did not waver.

"Did Tae truly arrange this—us?" Oddly shy, she studied the kaffiyeh in her hand, fallen from her hair, and then Faisal's face.

He smiled. "He told me he meant to find a safe place for you, whether he had to run from Umar's Hand or no."

"But he might have asked me." *You might.*

"He saw us when I took you to the scribe tent, and he said you smiled."

She flushed. "I but smiled at Sahar—"

Faisal touched her chin. "You love my hound of the dawn? That is good." He kissed the edge of her mouth and leaned his forehead against hers. "Yes, it was arranged," he said, his voice soft. "But do we not follow the path we wish?"

"I-I do wish it, but what we do touches so many—and Kyrin, I cannot leave her if she needs me."

"Ah, yes." He sighed and touched the back of her hand clutching the falcon brooch. "Does she yet stand between us?"

"Did you not give me her falcon pin? Do *you* not think of her?"

He blinked at her intensity. "My people make cloak pins in pairs. It seemed right you should have mine. I do think of our sister, but only of her at home across the sea."

Alaina bit her lip. "She is in danger, I think. Tae has not said much." *Did* Faisal truly love her, or after a time would their inner weaknesses and wounds drive them apart?

She knew what Nara would say. "Life moments are strange things. Often they must be taken apart like a bit of bad weaving, their threads repaired with forgiveness, and your heart reweave them in a moment of choice, a creation of understanding, and strong and loyal love."

Alaina gripped the brooch tight. Often feeling was the beginning of love. Loyalty and forgiveness took love deeper and higher. Choice perfected it. She hungered for that beginning, with Faisal. *But I still do not know for certain. . . I will not lie to him. I am afraid. Will he let me go if I must?*

A shadow moved outside the door behind Faisal. Alaina glimpsed Farook with a bundle of parchments. "Come in—" They were her parchments. Her words died when she saw his face, a red flush of guilt chased by pale fear. It was her Chronicle.

Parchment pages fluttered to the ground. Then Farook was gone on pounding feet.

8

The Judgment

Through knowledge the righteous will be delivered. ~ Proverbs 11:9

Sahar lay at Alaina's feet where she brushed her mare so as to be a little farther from Hafiz's sour-faced wife. Basimah watched her and Faisal distrustfully from the corner of the scribe's tent she had claimed to keep space between them. Cicero flanked Faisal, who worked furiously over the table in the tent. For all their working, neither she nor Faisal accomplished much.

There was little shade under the climbing sun. The warm smell of juniper and horse was sharp but not unpleasant. Sweat trickled down Alaina's back, horsehair and dirt gathered on her fingers. She could not keep her mind on the names for the mare she strove to recite. Salimah: safe, healthy? Salma: solace or comfort? Or would Shakira, thankful, fit her and what this sun saw? Alaina sighed. Most of the warriors were out hunting two-legged prey. She hoped for Farook's escape.

"We have him." A voice brought Alaina's head up. At the edge of camp, Tae dragged Farook toward them by the collar. Both were streaked with sweat and dirt; Farook was bareheaded and stumbling. "I found him near the Kathirib, a camp of five hundred," Tae said. "Who should not be there, with the peace."

Faisal had charged out of the scribe tent and now turned his head sharply toward Tae in disbelief. Tae pushed Farook to his knees before the prince.

Head and shoulders bowed, panting, Farook pulled his dagger in its sheath from his sash. He laid it before Faisal's feet, not raising his gaze.

Alaina left the mare's gleaming flank and found herself beside Faisal. Hafiz's wife dropped the wool thread she wove and flung herself inside the nearest tent, crying in a high voice, "Farook is caught; the prince will judge him! The slave has brought the Kathirib on us!" Alaina allowed herself a small smile as Basimah went from the empty tent on to the next. There were not many to hear. Most of the women were washing by the shaded pools.

Faisal's jaw worked. As if forced by unseen hands he bent and picked up Farook's blade. He unsheathed it. "I would not—have all witness this." His voice caught. He turned on Tae, savage. "Is it certain?"

"Yes, my prince." Tae was somber. "He was there, and the Kathirib, though he did not give us away. And they did not see us go. He did not break the peace." Tae turned so he could watch the approaches. "This is yours to judge."

Alaina's stomach roiled.

Faisal stared down at Farook without blinking, his fingers clenching and unclenching. He said, harsh and cold, "What words would you speak?"

Farook's breath stirred the dust. "Hafiz said if I did not find proof of your treachery to counter the ill Sarni's Chronicle wrought him, he would tell every warrior that you knew me a traitor, yet kept silent. So I did what he asked, but she knew." His head tilted toward Alaina's feet. "You had best kill me."

"Who *are* you? Whom do you serve?" Faisal's dark eyes bored into him.

"I am a slave of Sirius Abdasir, but your servant."

"Dare you say so? None can serve two masters."

Alaina flinched from the menace in Faisal's low growl.

Farook looked up, his eyes wet. "You came to hold my heart, my prince. I am glad you kept me close; I had no chance to get news to Zoltan."

Zoltan! Alaina found it hard to breathe. She dropped to her knees in front of Farook, keeping her hands from him with difficulty. "You dare name Zoltan guilty? He is no betrayer!"

"We are," Farook whispered. "The wazir held Nimah always within his reach. She is Zoltan's blood, and the heart of my heart." His voice quivered.

Alaina shuddered, her hand going to her throat. Sirius had held Tae hostage to force her and Kyrin to search for Hamal. It fit his pattern. It was irony, lifting Nimah to be keeper of his robes, then assigning her to serve his daughter. Had Nimah returned with Hala into more danger than in the desert?

But the peace was in place. The wazir's goal had been gained, Umar and his Hand turned back by Kyrin and Hala. Now there remained only Hafiz—Hafiz, who wielded Farook as his blade and set loose the power of fear among the Twilkets. But nearby there were five hundred Kathirib. Waiting. Who was the betrayer here? Had the peace already been broken?

"Your tongue has ever been straight," Faisal whispered. "You did not give us to the Kathirib?"

"No. I did not know they were there." Farook reached up to touch Faisal's hand and the haft of his dagger. "But with that many tents the Kathirib must be hunting us, peace or no peace. The blame for them will fall on you; your judgment must be seen to be just. They must not think you a traitor. If you forgive me, my prince, I can go from this earth in peace. Do what you must!"

Faisal's throat moved. His knuckles whitened about the hilt.

"I endanger your people!" Farook cried. "And you. If many believe Hafiz," he swallowed hard, "they will judge against me in the end." He drooped, spent, and his voice was muffled. "I would rather it be your hand."

Alaina swallowed. He did not deserve to die. Could she appeal to the sheyk? Beg Hafiz's mercy? Ask Tae to take Farook into the sands? Even steal Farook away herself? The mare threw up her head at far-off shouts. Basimah had found some to listen. They were coming.

Faisal gripped Farook's arms and jerked him to his feet.

"Now, I beg you!" Farook grabbed Faisal's shoulders and drew him close, the dagger bare between them. "I would not have that jackal's heart taste his triumph!"

"I cannot let him . . ." Faisal whispered, and bared his teeth and set the point of the blade to Farook's brown skin. Farook braced, staring into his prince's face.

Alaina said, swift and low, "Hafiz will not speak first of Farook's betrayal, for in the end Farook betrayed nothing. Together, our word may condemn Hafiz instead."

Her prince's arm quivered and his breath came fast. Farook did not look at her, waiting for his death.

She said quickly, "He used Farook against us in the matter of the parchments." Burn it—there was nothing for it but to lie to save a life. "My prince, tell your brothers how Farook ran in fear but returned to offer himself to your judgment—and also brought news of the lurking Kathirib. Tae caught him returning; is it not clear his heart is with you? Farook is a slave who thought better of his disobedience, who seeks to serve again in honor, bringing word of your enemies."

"Is this true?" Faisal's face was strained.

"No." Farook swallowed again. "I ran. I did not know the Kathirib were there, but I would not have returned. I should have faced you, about the parchments. But I never betrayed you, my prince."

Faisal's blade hand dropped. He cuffed Farook's arm. "I thought you endangered us all! But why did you not defend yourself?"

Farook's knees wavered, and he clutched at Faisal. Suddenly he laughed. "I did not think of the way out Sarni speaks of, only that Hafiz would use me against you."

"Fool!" Faisal shook him.

Tae's smile was so faint Alaina was uncertain of it.

Faisal helped Farook into the scribe tent and to a cushion, mindful of his stumbling feet. "Why did you run from us? It could not have been the parchments alone, I would never take a life for that."

"I—I saw Sarni, her hair. Not a scribe, but a woman, with you . . . and I had been in her tent, taking her Chronicle. With both judgments against me—" Farook glanced at Alaina, his face flaming. "I am full of sorrow. I will never darken your tent again, as Allah is my witness."

Faisal laughed, a short, joyous sound.

What did those gathering outside make of it? Alaina turned from the crowd and Tae's warding figure. She dropped the flap to touch Farook's arm. "I hold no ill will. And I am Sarni no longer. Doubtless Hafiz kept even this from you. I am Alaina Ilen."

Faisal shook Farook again and scowled at him, though a smile lurked beneath. "I hold ill will," he growled. "You will serve my Alaina and work to mend what you have taken. You will write, and sharpen quills, and she will teach you to read."

Farook's face fell for a bare instant.

Faisal added quickly, "For a time. Until Hafiz's tongue wearies of waiting to flay us. Then I will send you to the wazir with an invitation to Hala and Nimah to attend Alaina's days of henna."

He turned to smile at her. "My lark needs persuading that life in the desert with me has its own riches."

Alaina glared at him. She had not yet chosen, and he had agreed to give her time, until after the henna ceremony. But maybe he kept up the charade begun before the people. They had enough uncertainty to contend with.

Her prince ignored her brief glare and faced Farook, sober. "You will be to the wazir as you have been, but you will also report everything he speaks to me."

Farook paused, bowed his head, then grinned up at them. "My master and mistress are most gracious."

Outside, the clamor of many voices rose higher. Hafiz yelled over the crowd, "It is our right to know, if the Kathirib come!"

"Silence!" Tae barked. "The prince will speak of his decision when he wills."

Inside the tent, they looked at each other. The blood beat swiftly at the base of Farook's throat. "My prince, if you would mark me, as a sign of my near escape from your wrath, it might go easier for you." He tilted his head, baring his neck.

Faisal swallowed hard and set Farook's dagger in Alaina's hand. "You are the healer." He looked rather sick.

And being a healer made *her* accustomed to the blood of those she cared for? But she had not almost taken Farook's life. Alaina turned the blade and gripped Farook's warm skin.

He waited, quiet—not as young as he seemed. "No, tip your head toward me, to make the skin loose." She rolled her lip between her teeth. She must not cry, but steady her arm.

His finger on her wrist stopped her. "Mistress—it will but sting. I deserve the lash." The laughter in his eyes made her smile shakily, and her hand steadied.

Faisal fingered his chin, watching them from across the table. "You would die for me. You asked me to take your life three times."

Farook stiffened as the blade bit gently. Alaina lifted it away, and he stood, blood running down his neck in a fine line. There was fire in his eyes. "You are worthy."

Faisal inclined his head. "That is now the mark of your freedom. It is only just—brother."

A smile bloomed on Alaina's face. "Brother," she said softly. The same oath to them was in Farook's wordless gaze. He was no longer a slave. He had earned the prince's trust. Faisal had another man at his back, and it was well.

They walked out of the tent, Alaina moving to Faisal's right, Farook took his left, his blade returned to its sheath. In one glance Tae took in the thin wound across the side of Farook's neck. He knew what had passed, and much more.

Alaina wished all were as clear to her. Why were so many Kathirib gathered when the peace had been given, and the Hand recalled? And just how did Hafiz know Farook was the wazir's, though Farook never bore news to Zoltan?

The Twilket elders were quickly satisfied with Farook's witness. Against Tae, Alaina, and Faisal's word, even his own wife who witnessed Farook cast at the prince's feet, Hafiz could do nothing but keep accusations of treachery behind his teeth.

After dusk the scouts rode out. Warriors ate beside every fire, weapons ready.

Alaina caught Tae's elbow. He laid his last load—her blanket and rugs—down in the tent that had been Hala's. It was hers now. Until she chose. Faisal still waited for her, waited on her word. He could have any woman he wished, and yet he waited. He wanted her. That wanting seemed to hem her in. She pushed the thought away. "Tae, why did you not stop Faisal? He almost killed Farook. I do not understand."

Tae touched her shoulder and smiled. "I am proud of you, daughter. Your words to the prince prove you have grown. You thought quickly, with compassion. Yet Faisal must make his own decisions. And there was never much danger. He is a good man. As you are a good woman." He shrugged.

Alaina said quietly, "Yes, my father." He touched only her shoulder, a sign of the place she now held in another's heart. She would show him the same courtesy. But she felt far outside of herself, far from everyone, as if her spirit fled into the desert, into the sand and darkness, to hide and not be found. There, her words could never be a danger, written or spoken.

Tae's smile faltered. He cupped her cheek in his rough-skinned hand. "My daughter, you are of my heart's blood and you will always be so. Meet me at the pools at first light." His face hardened. "The Kathirib come. It is almost certain. Your staff will add the strength you need for the touch of death. I was wrong. You will prove me so by learning well."

"Yes, my father." Alaina grinned. She was to know the death touch, with the staff as a tool. The thought did not quite bring the elation she had thought it would, but it was not his fault her heart was torn. On impulse she kissed his cheek. "Your Huen waits. You are also a worthy man."

Tae studied her and then inclined his head, a man's bow to a woman. One side of his mouth turned up. He turned away, wiping at his eyes, and walked into the desert.

A full moon rode the sky. Alaina held out her arms and spun in the warm wind, thankful. *'You are my heart's blood.'* It was not a night the Kathirib would attack. And a prince gave her freedom to choose.

9

Mahr and Henna

You who seek God, let your heart revive. ~ Psalm 69:32

The Kathirib camp of five hundred had melted, mist under the sun, and a heavy rain had concealed their escape from the force Tae and Faisal led after them. No one had seen sign of an enemy since, and the Kathirib would never attack again so soon. So Hafiz persuaded his sheyk.

Alaina sniffed. Tae continued his forays in the dawn with a few old men. He refused to let Faisal come with them. The scar on Farook's neck had healed, and the monsoon rains were near their end. Sahar's pups were twelve hands of days old. And with the rains almost over, Hafiz argued to bring the far-flung Twilket sentries home to witness their prince's wedding.

"Mistress! The honored daughter of the wazir has come!" Farook panted out the news inside the door of her tent, his eyes alight. "She brings Nimah and two others to attend you."

Hala had arrived for the days of henna. Did she bring any news of Kyrin? They had promised to write, each to the other.

It was not Farook's doing that her thoughts scattered. Alaina made her smile sincere. "It is well, Farook. Doubtless you have much to speak of with Zoltan. Might our prince's guests need a hand with their beasts?" At her shooing motion, Farook grinned and dashed back out.

Alaina sighed. She would be washed and groomed and suffer hours of stillness on the morrow while henna was applied in intricate designs from hand to elbow, toe to knee and then allowed to dry. She would be wrapped and bound rather like an Egyptian mummy. Trapped—it brought to mind the wet hide of punishment Umar would have wound her in, and the tickling brush in her hand became for a moment the feet of scurrying ants. But she was not bound. Alaina set the brush down with a decisive smack.

The winter air was warm with promise of spring. Her skin still prickled. What henna designs would fit a prince's bride? Flowers and vines and leaves, something besides the ugly line-on-line motifs some favored. She hungered to please Faisal with the beauty of the henna. Though she would be more comfortable with Nara than Hala.

Nara's motherly twinkle could disperse wisps of night thoughts as if they had never been. As Ali's erstwhile cook, who now served the wazir, Nara had championed her and her sister from the first, when they were newly brought captive into Ali's house. Nara would treat her simply as a woman, not one sought for her influence with a prince, for her skill in herbs, or for her scribe's talent for trouble. Simply a woman. Alaina reached up. Her new *hattah* did not flatten her hair, set lightly on her head as Bedouin maidens wore the material, folded much as the men's kaffiyeh but without the head cord. Though she still let her hair loose when she could. What would Faisal say if he saw her so? Would he think her too unmaidenly, too strong? Why was it so hard for her to choose her prince?

A pup stirred, pushing against the nest of her lap in a sleepy stretch. Alaina's mouth quirked. Sahar's seven pups quickly grew from stumbling awkwardness toward their swift heritage. Sahar had every right to stand tall and proud as she and Cicero flanked Alaina and Faisal at their pups' presentation to the other salukis of the hunt last even.

At the moment, oblivious of such an honor, various wet puppy noses and tongues tickled her ankles and toes. The smallest pup was black as desert night, with a star of white on his forehead. Four were sandy colored above and cream beneath, and there was a male as red as his mother. Alaina tickled an ear, flicked a sandy tail, and stroked a soft head resting on her thigh.

The largest female pup was washed by Cicero's moon-shadow and silver, even down her shapely, muscled legs, with a lighter color beneath. The lightest blush of dawn touched the tip of her tail and brows. Her will showed signs of matching Kyrin's.

But Kyrin would not leave guests waiting overlong. Alaina rose, gently dislodging the saluki pups. With a last stroke for Cicero's daughter, she hurried out. Would the pups be just as oblivious to a handfasting? Sahar looked after her and whined.

§

Alaina led Hala, Nimah, and the other women back to her tent. Alaina hid her smile when Nimah's gaze followed Farook, who strode past them with the baggage mounts. She sobered. She faced the same decision. Where was it safe to lay one's heart?

In the door of her tent, with a face sour as a green persimmon, Basimah shooed Cicero and his playful, tumbling brood out past the ropes. One of the pups leaped to clear the camel-hide cord, tangled with it, and fell. He rose snorting in a cloud of dust.

Alaina struggled against her smile. The red pup was learning about people, camels' feet, and bushes. He discovered that a jump from a scribe's table was one thing and a leap over a tent rope, another. He might earn the name Dart. Yet, burn it, that Basimah! She needn't chase them off. Alaina sighed.

Did she secretly wish for the power to burn what opposed her? She had not meant to let "burn it" pass her lips again.

"Oh!" Hala knelt to stroke the smallest gamboling pup. "He's a very noble one, isn't he? He looks like a night star."

"Yes." It seemed another pup was making himself a name. Alaina swallowed her ire and nodded to Basimah. After all, the pup was whole, and it was soon to be her wedding night, for all Basimah knew. The woman glared at her and hurried away.

Alaina shook off her ill will and turned to Hala with a smile. "He is from the prince's Sahar and my sister's Cicero. Nightstar is a good name. I am sure Zoltan would be happy to have him in your father's kennels."

"Truly?" Hala glowed. "Thank you, Alaina. That is a queenly gift! I will treasure him." Hala picked him up and let the growling pup worry at her sleeve a moment, then gave him a last pat and put him down, to link her arm in Alaina's. Her smile was secretive. "Come, I've brought you what the prince asked for." She pulled Alaina inside her tent.

In moments Nimah and the other two serving women carried inside a veritable stack of henna pots and bowls. And after them, wraps, handmade design applicators, kohl, and perfumes.

She reached out a wondering hand and drew back hastily. Delicate jars and vials were arranged on the table. No room for a scribe's elbows there. Likewise no room for a prince's. Or for a pup's scrambling paws.

Soon gauzy veils and white thawbs draped over one woman's arms. There were robes of earth colors and jewel tones, in silk, cotton, and wool swathes across Alaina's sleeping blankets and heaped on the rugs. It was a bazaar in miniature, as if she were a merchant in a souk. Alaina swallowed hard. Kyrin would love it, for all her joy in the way of the warrior. As would she, if it did not represent—what?

Resplendent in a dark blue thawb and gold trim, with a blue bead pendant on her brow, Hala turned gracefully and laid her aba aside. Her eyes gleaming with excitement, she clapped her hands.

One of her women, giggling, held out before Alaina a double handful of rings and necklaces of amber and jet stones, along with chains of polished coins. The other woman, her eyes bright within a thick border of kohl, presented in her cupped hands a stack of armlets, bracelets, and anklets in a careful tower. Then Hala uncovered a polished bronze mirror as high as her waist with a flourish.

Alaina stopped, rooted in the middle of the tent, her mouth open. Faisal gave her all this? She found herself fingering the simple amber falcon that pinned her cloak at her shoulder in the way of Britannia.

"The prince has said you are to have the best *mahr* he can give," Hala said, "and the freshest henna for the starkest tint. Mey will come with the next sun to reveal your henna design to complement your bright hair." Her impish smile turned mischievous. "Nimah and I cannot paint the henna for we are not joined to a man, but Mey is happily married. We would not bring ill luck to you."

Alaina shook her head, caught between a frown and a laugh. "What does luck have to do with the design of the Master of the Stars? Your caring hands bring me no ill." If it *was* his design that she ride beside a desert prince, on a mare of no name.

A look passed between the women. "We may not cast aside tradition . . ."

Alaina could not keep back her smile. "Have you *looked* at the stars, my sisters? Their Master calls them by name and keeps each in its course." If only she could feel his warding hand of protection and guidance this moment.

"Then it shall be as you say." Hala pursed her lips. "But Mey will begin your pattern and mix the paste; she knows the best oils and the greenest henna powder."

Alaina smiled and held out her hands. "You have my thanks, Hala. Forgive my frown. I am so glad you have come! This mahr . . ." She fingered a delicate silver ring like a curled twig, with a tiny leaf in the middle. "This calls to my heart." A branch cut off to form a ring of eternity, it held new life. She slipped it on and studied her hand. The ring was cool and bright. It may well have come from Britannia, when Ali raided Kyrin's stronghold and took her and Kyrin from all they knew. Alaina clenched her hand into a fist.

"Then it is yours. Do not forget they come in twos."

Alaina picked up the second ring. "Faisal did not send *all* this, did he? He must not beggar himself. My bride-price is not so high." Did he seek her hand so, laden with gold and silver? It was not like him.

"He wanted you to have your choice of—" Hala began.

But Nimah broke in, "Oh no, Alaina, all the women of the house wanted to add a piece of their own mahr to the prince's, to wish you riches and a long life. See, this anklet is from Nara." She held up a thick gold band hung with tiny, tinkling silver coins from the pile. "This will fit you well. And this!" She picked up a gold bracelet set with green stones.

A sob welled in Alaina's throat for the women in bonds she had laughed with. "They remembered me," she whispered. Faisal revealed her old bonds in Ali's former household, and reforged them, but this time in joyful memory. This was a bond without fear, the difference between the chains of slavery and love.

Hala seated herself on a cushion and raised her brow. "Yes, they do remember. How could they forget? Qadira recites your poetry, she's gathered your verses in a book. Nimah tells me stories of you. I am almost sad you escaped my father, for then I would have a sister." She laughed and looked away. "My father hates the sea since its waves parted him and Hamal when he left. I told my father of Kyrin's dagger, for I wondered why she had my cousin's blade. But my father waved his hand and said, 'It is an oath between us.'" Hala shrugged. "It is as well he has a faithful bodyguard with him now. Umar will banish my father's sorrowful spirit, for he lives to serve his wazir." Her wry face lightened. "Oh, and a man named Kaish bears a letter from the Kathirib for your Sheyk Gershem. It bears the caliph's seal. The peace is written."

She tugged Alaina down beside her and spread a parchment on her knee. "See? My father sent you this. A writ for Kyrin's freedom, and you are to witness it." Her hand shook the slightest bit.

Alaina's mind raced even as her hand closed convulsively on the missive. The falcon dagger again. Could she trust it? Could she trust the wazir? What oath with the wazir did it signify, beyond Kyrin's promise to find Hamal? They were words of peace, of peace with the Kathirib. And words of freedom.

Hala cleared her throat and intoned in her sweet, light voice, with a grand sweep of her arm, "When the winds permit his ships to anchor, the wazir requests that you and Tae Chisun sign this writ, in your land where he will honor Kyrin Cieri and speak of beginning trade with Britannia." She lowered her voice. "If you both come the honorable wazir will be assured of Tae Chisun's goodwill. Then your warrior in exile will enjoy the caliph's favor, and escaped slaves will not be spoken of. Say you will, Alaina. Then you will see your people, and Kyrin. And I would not be alone there again, no matter what my father gains in trade." Hala's face bore a worn look.

"Oh, Hala." Alaina drew her hand in both of hers, holding back tears. Hala had lost so much more than she. "I will go, if I can." If only Hala knew how much she wished it.

A tear slid down Hala's face, followed by another, her eyes wells of sadness. She wiped her cheek hastily. "You are to be wed, I should have no tears. Forgive me."

Nimah laid her hand on Hala's knee, her mouth trembling. The other women looked at the floor, downcast.

Abruptly Alaina felt savage. "What else *ought* you to do? Men can be dogs. What has been ripped from you will not return. Mourn it." She leaned forward. "But after that grieving is past, ask the Master of the Stars. And he will give you a heart to live as he wills, and new dreams. That bit of pierced flesh is only a sign of something greater within you, something that you never surrendered."

Hala blinked at her, with a wet catch of breath. "What do you mean?"

"Your virgin purity remains in your heart. You are not at fault."

Hala drew a trembling breath and straightened. "That is true."

"It is also not quite certain I shall wed." Alaina grimaced. "Though our prince is most generous and kind."

The women stared at her. Hala's mouth was a circle of surprise.

Alaina's face heated. "I will ask the Master of all to help me see my way, for Kyrin is closer to me than blood. I will not be bound by less than love." *My path divides again. And I am afraid.*

They looked uncertainly at each other. "Love?" Hala's laugh was not quite bitter. "You have it. I can see it in him. I hope you find that joy."

Alaina wished she could be as certain, and said nothing. It would not be kind to handfast him if she could not give him all.

Hala said earnestly, "But you say I may have new dreams also. Will you speak to him, this Master of the Stars, who is a Father to me?"

"Yes. But Hala, he loved you before he made the foundation of the world, you know. He hears *your* heart." *And my uncertain one.*

"Come, let us ask him for wisdom," said Nimah. "Once his daughter, always his daughter."

Alaina clasped hands with her and Hala, and the other women tentatively joined in. Nimah's voice rose softly as they bowed their hearts before the Master of the Stars. By cleansing tears released at last, Alaina broke the circle of her sisters. She reached for Hala and kissed her forehead.

Hala was quiet, in the grip of wonder. She was held by the hands of the Master and Father who loved her more than any earthly father ever could. New life was ahead. He would never let her soul go back to darkness and death.

Alaina's fingers trembled. How could such joy and pain fill the same moment, in hearts side by side? Somehow, she saw bonds and danger in her own future, though her heart leaped when her prince smiled or touched her hand. He also thought to wed her was needed for their people. Despite the peace with the Kathirib.

Alaina laid the wazir's letter on the table. What was in her own heart? She must either leave Faisal, or Kyrin. Her throat ached, and she felt a growing urge to hit something. She gripped her fist over her stomach. The rings bit into her hand.

That moment, Basimah ducked into the tent. With a disapproving look at Alaina's wet face, she set down a heavy platter of food on the low table. Hala thanked her for her hospitality, and Basimah smiled and wished her blessings and went out again.

"Ah hah, something to strengthen us!" Nimah pounced on the platter with a gamin grin. While they ate cakes and camel milk with dates, Nimah said around a satisfied mouthful, "It is good Umar is not here. Tears make him call for his whip." One of the women coughed on a laugh.

Hala raised her head swiftly. "Umar is *mine* now. I would never give him leave to do so." There was new fire in her eye.

Alaina twisted the silver ring about her finger, against its twin. If she refused Faisal, would Hala perhaps find happiness with him? Might Hala heal his heart and let her go back to Britannia? Unhappiness choked her. She felt she must see Kyrin before she wed. Was it simple fear or something more?

But it *was* good Umar was not here yet. When he came for the feast, should she pretend as if the days he hunted her had never been? Ought she to impress on him the power of her alliance with the prince of the Twilkets?

Either could be dangerous. Umar was near the wazir's ear. But he was not here. Not yet. And Hafiz—he was quelled for the moment, as Basimah made clear by her resentment.

Alaina turned her mind to Nimah's happy chatter. "I will paint Cicero's tail and paws with henna, for he must celebrate his mistress's day of gladness, too."

Hala rose lithely to her feet. *"I* will henna the prince's horse."

"His name is Zahir." Alaina smiled to cover her sudden urge to shake Hala. Where had that feeling come from? Her alliance with Faisal was not yet certain. She was equally certain none but she would henna Sahar's paws and tail and adorn the pups. Nimah and the others' voices faded in her ears. Would a stylized juniper sprig or desert iris be best? The henna pattern should be a sigil of both houses. She rather thought the iris fitting. A symbol of life—bound together by a lance and quill. The iris grew in both her land and his. The ruffled petals would contrast delicately with the edged tools of the warrior and the scribe. Or ought it to be a wolf's head?

Alaina swallowed the last bit of her date. She could imagine joining her life to Faisal. Nothing would be the same without Kyrin, but all *would* be well. Those around her would make her coming three sunrises before her true henna night, when she pledged herself to another, joyful.

Alaina's breath came faster. If she stayed, she would see Shahin and the rest of the Aneza rejoice, whom Tae had invited for the third day of the wedding feast.

Faisal left her free, so why did she fear their hand-fasting, yet also fear if she turned away, she turned her back on her one chance of a good life? *Master of the Stars, I do not know what to do.*

In Ali's house her life had been full of rosewater, embroidering priceless thawbs, performing the warrior's art with Kyrin, scribing, and dreaming of the caliph's court and freedom. Then she fled to the desert, practiced healing, and wielded a quill of dishonor among the Twilkets. Not the renown she had wished, as Hafiz could attest. Alaina grimaced.

Somehow she'd learned to love the silence and majesty of Araby, the wadis, the wide spaces. It gave her a twist of heart. How long had it been since she picked up a needle? Her smile twitched. Even Basimah must acknowledge that skill.

Once, no *if*, she was joined to Faisal, the needle might never leave her hand after the women discovered her prowess with it. There. Her mind betrayed her again. Alaina buried her face in a fading bunch of irises in a flagon on the table. Farook had gathered it for her this morn. Odd, how the desert iris was so much sweeter than rosewater. It had a perfume all its own.

How could she write Kyrin, dearer than breath, and say that another path had caught her feet and she wanted to walk it? She could not be a scribe to Kyrin in Britannia *and* wife to an Araby prince. Had her sister's letter of reply gone astray over the passing moons? Surely by now Kyrin's father had dealt with the unruly lords. Maybe the missive would come soon.

The Kathirib, Kyrin, the peace, and the falcon blade would have to settle into events as the Master of the Stars ordered. Without her, for the moment.

"Alaina, have you heard a word we've said?" Nimah was exasperated.

"Of course. I cannot disappoint you." Alaina smiled. "I will paint my henna sigil on the back of your hands, with graceful dots down the fingers. Nimah, you and Mey can sketch the designs and take my mind from my forebodings."

"Yes," chimed in Hala, "and dream of Faisal, desert wolf, prince and protector of his own."

The following dawn, Alaina woke sweating and tangled in her blankets. Her heart pounded and her mouth was dry parchment. She had to get out. She staggered up. The mare would carry her far away, until she cast off the last clinging of the night. At the edge of the wadi, where sweet iris and small yellow lilies grew in the damp earth, Alaina dropped from the mare's back. She sat on a rock near a wide patch of flowers, breathing deep. She smiled at the screech of mountain parakeets. They could be no louder or prouder than the cockerels of Britannia.

Restlessly, she mounted again and turned toward the desert in the coolness. The sun's first rays streamed over the hills. Nothing should be wrong on such a day.

10

Desire and Danger

My heart will not fear, though war arise. ~ Psalm 27:3

Chill sand, quiet rock and dune, the full-throated paean of a sand-lark, a herd of reem, hooves tapping, their horns sharp and dark as they trotted away after a liquid-eyed gaze at her on the mare: everything in this land pulled at something inside her. It was a piercing shard of longing and joy, not quite a comfortable ache. The scent of morning earth in shadow and sun, the clear, bright horizon, stirred a tingle through her.

Alaina patted her mare's smooth shoulder, already sweaty, and sniffed the horsey salt-smell on her fingers. She should be thinking of rosewater, of Britannia and Kyrin, of her answer. Even the lack of the duties she would have had in Ali's house.

"So, Sarni, how is it?"

Alaina straightened with a jerk and her knees tightened. The mare reared. When she came down, Alaina had her staff across the saddle, her hands whitening on the wood.

Faisal sat Zahir on the dune beside hers, Cicero lying at ease beneath his bare feet, tongue lolling. How long had they been watching her?

The feathers of the prince's lance fluttered above his head. His mouth quirked up on one side. The sun shadowed his face, glowing around him.

Her thoughts fled, bumping, tangling. Her tongue tied itself in a knot. What was it about him that made her reach for words, as if he moved beyond the meanings of the ones she knew? It took her two tries to secure her suddenly awkward staff in the carrying thongs. "It's been blessedly quiet," she mumbled, "until now."

The skin of Faisal's jaw tightened, and he reined Zahir about.

"I—I did not mean that ill."

He stopped, waiting. What was he doing, riding the sands with bare feet? Soon the sand would burn. "I, I mean the desert has—a peace about it. It used to be empty, now it is not." Her face flamed. "I don't mean since you are here, but the reem, the flowers—" Was she a scop or a baboon without hope of words? She dug her hole deeper and deeper.

Zahir circled down from his dune, seemingly without Faisal's direction. The prince stopped beside her with a shift of weight in his cloth saddle. Damp sand clung to his toes. He grinned. "Come, I want to show you something."

He kicked Zahir, and the stallion shot over the top of the dune as if they were of one mind.

Alaina drew a deep breath of desert air and leaned forward. "Go, sweet one." The mare raced after Zahir, her mane whipping Alaina's cheeks. One end of her hattah loosed, flapping over her shoulder. She reached up and pulled it free, stuffing the length in her sash. The wind trailed strong fingers through her hair. She molded herself along the mare's back, grinning. This was to live.

Faisal leaned low over Zahir's neck, lance close-held to his flank. He pulled up too soon for Alaina, and she brought the mare dancing in beside them.

The prince pointed. "The fierce lightning of the first rains foretold it. See? They grow where the bolts strike."

Alaina peered at the thin grass scattered over the sand. There was nothing else. No, the earth was cracked, and pushing up along the widest cracks, like pale rough rocks arranged by a child were—truffles. It could not be. Here? In the sere sands?

Faisal grinned again, dropped down and began to dig. *"Fagaa.* Desert truffles. Very good. And good for my grandfather's blood."

Alaina dismounted and knelt beside him. The truffles varied from the size of a coin to some as large as her palm, roughly round in shape. She knew their healthful properties were strong and widely applied, from eye infections to unwanted growths. She wet her lips, watching him dig, his hands deft and sure, without hesitation. "Faisal, I—you have to know." She stared at the back of his hand, at the brown skin stretched over thin tendon and bone. "I am a healer *because* blood sickens me. Kyrin does not mind it. I have never fought to blood, for all that I know the warrior's arts. If you would hand-fast me," she changed her focus to an innocuous mushroom, for she dared not look at him, "you must know I am not a warrior as you or Tae. And it is hard for me to choose—things." *Anything. For fear of—of hurt. And you are a wolf of the desert.* "It seems I am something between maidenly and strong, so I am neither."

Silence. She dared glance up.

Faisal sat back on his heels, his sandy hands on his knees. He did not smile at her weak words, his brown eyes deep. He said quietly, "I know. I remember Farook." And very gently, "Alaina, what fear binds you? More than blood and Kyrin hold you back.

Can you call its name, and overcome its fear in the living air? You are a healer, a scribe, a scop. I know you are strong."

Alaina plucked one of the damp, rubbery fagaa from the disturbed earth before his knees and turned it in her fingers. It was hard to speak. But if they were to belong to each other their words should link them. *Burn it. No—let the true words grow, be what they are meant to be, not hide behind others.* She blurted, "I think I fear where our path will lead if I choose before I know Kyrin is well. Also, I fear the unknown. I do wish to be with you, to please you." The words were hot with choking misery. "But everything turns to dust when I grip it."

Faisal sighed, a long sigh, his smile sudden and quick. "Such things are also in my mind. Will I please you? Camels, dates, and milk, a tent: those I have. My protection, my heart and mahr are yours. All of these—if you choose them." He swallowed, looked away and back.

Then touched her silver ring with the tip of a finger. "This pleases you?" He was almost shy.

"Yes." Her heart lifted. Faisal could laugh. He was steadfast. He had the strength of a lion and a deep love for the Master of the Stars at his core. He risked as much with her as she did with him. Their growing together would be hard at times, but it would be good. Yes, it could be. Kyrin must understand. Alaina pressed her lips together.

As if he heard her thought, Faisal said, "You ought to scribe a letter to Kyrin, whichever path you take." He looked across the sand. "Your sister may rejoice. It is my thought Kyrin would rejoice for us." He swallowed hard.

Alaina smiled but her lips trembled and her throat felt thick. Kyrin would sacrifice anything for her. Would risk, had risked, all. Her sister by hearth and salt and blood. But divided from her by sands and seas, she had grown to love another, in a different way.

And the Master of all said it was good. Alaina laid her hand in Faisal's. His fingers closed around hers, no more a trap but a hedge of protection. They could grow together.

"Yes," Alaina whispered, "I choose your heart."

Faisal jerked around to look at her. Then he laughed in wonder and growing belief. "My Alaina." Tears glittered in his eyes. He swept her to him and his wiry warmth enfolded her.

She kissed him. The end of his turban tickled her nose, and she sneezed, and their laughter rose together. Then they were laughing so hard they rolled over the fagaa, unheeding. When they sat up at last her heart was light, and she heard the same lightness in his voice and smiled at him.

She brushed sand from her cheek; a bit of fagaa hung over his ear. She reached to smooth it away. He caught her hand and held it in his, and Alaina leaned her head against him with a sigh. His heart thudded under her ear. He whispered something she did not have to hear to understand.

Ah, Master of the Stars, you do all things well. Alaina smiled, then straightened with a jerk. "Oh! Hala and Nimah, the others . . ."

She scrambled to her feet, and Faisal followed. They grinned at each other. There was no need for words. They swung to their horses' backs and walked them toward the pools for their morning drink, keeping the dunes between them and camp. What they shared was not yet for other eyes. They passed from the sands to gravel plain and saw, stretching across it, the long arm of the mountain ridge that shielded the pools.

A hiss, a thud, and a plume of dust rose beside Zahir. An arrow protruded from the ground, its feathers dull grey. "What—"

"Tae," Faisal breathed. Then he was down and had the arrow and her mare's rein in his hand, turning the horses to face the mountain to make them a smaller target.

Alaina slid down and freed her staff. Her mare between her and the mountainside, she scanned the crest and downward. Nothing moved. Cicero raised his head, eyes and nose questing. The steep side was dry rock and gravel with grey-green juniper, scattered tamarisk, and a few wild fig trees. She would be comforted to see any sign of Tae. But if she could, so could any lurking enemy.

There was a bundle at the tip of the arrow. Faisal plucked free the scrap of hide. He said low and fast, "The Kathirib come. Tae says some may be at the pools already. Or watching camp. They may be watching us. He waits to see and follow. He has sent out others. He asks us to give nothing away."

Faisal's mouth flattened as he nudged Zahir into a walk. Alaina followed. If they were watched it was too late, their alarm had been noted. Howling raiders could descend any moment.

They walked parallel to the mountain, Faisal's eyes darting everywhere. "It's a short ride to camp. If they are not in sight yet, they will hear our horses if we run. Until we part, we must pretend to see and hear nothing." He looked tensely at the mountain. "I will find Tae, and you must warn the sheyk. If you see any movement, Alaina, ride hard. Give the alarm before they attack. They may come down behind the tents also, by the wadi."

They neared an outcrop of three standing stones between camp and the mountain's foot.

Faisal tugged Zahir's head around and thumped the base of his neck with his fist. At the signal, Zahir's rear legs folded, then his front knees. Faisal stepped free of the saddle, his lance in his hand. A second arrow thudded into a rock and skittered away.

Alaina jerked around, every muscle taut. But it was another of Tae's arrows. She must not notice. "There, a reem. See?" She pointed back the way they had come, as the gazelle that had been watching them bounded away. She let out her breath.

Pulling her startled, sidling mare back beside Zahir with an effort, Faisal gritted between his teeth, "Tae wishes us to go on, but he must not watch our backs alone. He needs me, and those in camp. By the Djinn!" Faisal exploded, striking the saddle with his fist, "I can make no move that does not appear a dog's cowardly expedience! At least to those like Hafiz. But better my name than my men's blood." He glanced longingly at the ridge. "Tae is worth ten of Hafiz. He will have the first Kathirib that reach him fleeing for their mothers."

Alaina drew a deep breath. "My prince, you are our sheyk, though none have named you so. The Kathirib may think none have seen them—as we have not." For all intents and purposes, Faisal *was* their only sheyk. *Help him, Master of the Stars, be humble enough to hear your counsel.*

He snorted, and remounted. Zahir also snorted, and the mare nuzzled his glossy black neck. Alaina gained her mare's back. Her hands were cold despite the sun. Their horses' hooves thudded over gravel and rock and finally earth. The stillness of rock, tree, and the steadily greying sky loomed around them. They continued on their heedless course it seemed for an age.

Alaina heard nothing, saw nothing, but the occasional shush of Cicero's paws on rock, the horses' hooves on earth and their alert ears. She kept her staff in her hand.

If attacked she would strike whatever target came first, whether the blow killed or no, in the quickest way to stop her attacker. A blow could kill if it were applied to the temple, to the throat, to the eye, or to the back of the head. Or the heart—if a blow came heavy and hard enough—up under the diaphragm or through the ribs. Tae had known a man strong enough to do so with a hand blow: to shock a man's innards so his blood beat did not start again. But if an enemy was senseless they were not a threat. She frowned. Until they woke.

Tae sent no more arrows. Faisal's scowl died into sober watchfulness. She and Faisal paced on.

Sweat ran down her back. No clash of lance or shouts disturbed the growing heat. All was quiet, a heaviness growing in the air. Alaina's skin crawled. When might riders thunder up around them, or an arrow thud into their backs? It took all her will not to look back.

Her hair tickled her cheek. She gathered it up and donned her hattah. She must keep the Kathirib thinking them out riding together. A prince and the one he loved.

"Now we run." Faisal looked across Zahir's neck at her, his face tense. They were out of the protective reach of the best archer on the mountain. "Let them think we race."

She nodded. "If we race, then let us win the prize." A smile touched his mouth, and she laid her hand on his arm. "May Cicero carry our hearts ahead?" Wolf-like, Faisal grinned, and a word sent Cicero streaking before them.

They leaped into motion. Alaina leaned close over the mare's mane. Rising wind whipped the strands into her face. Dust drove along the ground under her mare's feet and stung her skin. A storm to match the doings of this day.

She met Faisal's gaze. A quick, hot shaft of anger and hope, it held a bit of sadness. She smiled at him fiercely and kicked the mare harder. They must reach the tents.

Neck and neck, they thundered to the edge of camp. Alaina pulled up before her tent, while Faisal trotted Zahir toward Gershem and Hafiz's. Nimah peered out in amazement.

"Nimah! Where is Hala? Get her, you must leave! Farook and Kentar will go with you—"

Nimah stammered, "She is with Mey and Basimah, they went to get more oil for your henna. The tea tree is good for—"

"Forget the oil! Grab your waterskins, Hala's good aba, and your thickest thawb. A storm comes, and with it, the Kathirib. They must not find the wazir's daughter. No man can get her again!"

Nimah paled and jerked back inside. Alaina swung the mare away. To be scop to her people in the coming conflict she needed the quills; paper and parchment; an oiled skin; a dagger for cutting, and ink from the scribe's tent. Dust was thick now in the warm, close air, the horizon greyer.

Faisal's people—her people—swarmed about the tents like a kicked anthill. A child wailed, clinging to a warrior's legs. The boy's mother pulled him away and lifted him. He clung to her neck, his small head nestled beside hers. His father laid a hand on his curls then turned away.

Alaina kicked the mare into a trot, dodging them. This was not a raid where life-blood was avoided, where all fought for plunder. The truffles she and Faisal had picked were forgotten, of a piece with the quiet morn.

Farook met her at the scribe tent with a sack of bread and dates and a skin of milk. "The prince sent these, and this message." He straightened to his tallest and said in stern imitation, "Tell her to stay back from the battle, to be scop to our people." Farook looked at her. "What is a scop?"

She dismounted swiftly. "A speaker, a scribe." Her breath came short as she packed the things Farook brought in the mare's saddle bags. He handed her a fistful of quills. "A scop is a recorder of life, Farook. A historian." He looked blank. "One who records the deeds of her people." His face brightened. She must watch them all, and record every act of bravery and courage. Sighing, she added, "A shaper of stories." For those who lived to hear them.

She needed a high place where she could watch. The women would be gathering the goats, camels, and spare horses to the place Tae had appointed. She would not have to fight, but it would be hard to wait and watch.

Farook nodded soberly. "I go to loose Truthseeker for the prince. Take this." He set a parchment-wide piece of wood, slender, sheathed in hardened sinew in her hands. A scribing table of a size she might carry with her.

"My thanks." She tucked it under her arm. "Guard Hala and Nimah."

"With my life. Do you guard yours, beloved of my prince."

11

Forge of Hearts

Like an eagle that swoops on its prey. ~ Job 9: 26

Alaina panted up the ridge outside the wadi, leading her mare under the flickering shadows of racing clouds. The rock-and-earth banks Tae had raised across the wadi above the pools to stop just such an attack, had proved too strong an obstacle . The Kathirib went around.

Wind swirled the smell of rock and warm juniper about her, stirred her blue Persian trousers, tight at the ankle, and flapped her dark hip-length tunic. Her hattah pulled oddly on her hair, hastily twisted up in a bun beneath it and held by Tae's hair sticks in the manner of the women of his people.

Far below, the Kathirib approached the ridge in a white-robed mass, across the plain she and Faisal had fled. Amid rising dust, the distant figures in kaffiyeh and turban with winking lances and scattered pennons shouted, their voices faint. Blades were raised, and round shields hung on saddles.

Alaina's booted foot thumped hot rock, not yet cooled by the clouds. She turned, panting for breath. Her lungs and legs burned. She steadied herself against a wide juniper clinging to the steep hillside, papery bark beneath her hand. A boulder rose from the ground two strides off. Another rock before it made a flat enough table. The position gave good cover and a spanning view of the plain.

The mare whuffled behind her. "Shhh, *Etain.*" The mare's name came to her early on the climb, though there were none to hear, halfway up the ridge. Alaina fastened Etain's rein about the tree and tugged. Her horse held much of the elfin about her, in both her name and her sparkling eye. Something of Britannia and of Kyrin. Etain's warm, soft nose was a comfort. Alaina found her quill and ink and laid them on the rock atop Farook's scribing board.

Mounted two deep before the base of the ridge, Gershem's Twilket warriors waited, clad in earth-colored thawbs. They presented an ordered front to their enemy, who gathered to fight in the usual way: mounted warriors eager to descend in chaotic madness on their enemies until they overwhelmed them.

Zahir walked out to meet the Kathirib line, head up, tail arched, hooves dancing. The afternoon light was interspersed by clouds that ran across the plain, forerunners of the approaching storm. Sun and shadow raced around her prince.

Why must *he* speak with the Kathirib? Hafiz wanted her prince's place, and yet he let him approach their enemies alone. As a foreign warrior, it was impolitic for Tae to treat with the Kathirib. And Gershem must not fall. As Faisal said, if his grandfather fell, the Twilkets would weaken, divided in mind and heart.

Slender and straight, all in black, with a pale kaffiyeh, the prince was one with the stallion. He carried his shield at his knee, lance in hand, sword sheathed. He was within Kathirib bowshot.

Without taking her gaze from Faisal, Alaina sat and reached for her parchment. Where was the jackal-eaten thing? Her throat scratched from the hot dust, and she ached for her staff.

She hoped none of the Kathirib contemplated treachery. Her fumbling fingers found the smooth skin, and she loosened her fingers so she would not break the white quill.

Practice on parchment, perfect on paper . . . Tae's wisdom. Now he held the middle of the Twilket line with Gershem. On the sheyk's left, Hafiz sat motionless on his blood bay at the end of the line. Faisal would hold the far right. When he returned. Between the savage banks of glistening lances, shields, and swords, wielded by fiercer men, Faisal raised his arm.

Alaina held her breath. She could not see the sand streaming from his hand in the sign of peace. Would she see more than a flutter of Hala's letter the prince held? He meant to challenge the Kathirib, ask why they broke the caliph's peace, dishonored the caliph's seal.

A man in red with a black turban urged his horse from the white-robed line to meet her prince. Was it his colors of blood and burning that made his face seem paler than those of his men around him? Something about the man nagged at her. She leaned forward, the rock before her digging into her knees.

A camel-length from Faisal, the Kathirib leader lifted the tip of his lance. Then he kicked his horse into a gallop. Alaina gasped. Faisal raised his weapon and urged Zahir forward. They passed with a soundless shock.

The man bent back, struck through—no, Faisal's lance had carried off the warrior's black turban. His hair blazed up, a torch of ashy light as he reeled in the saddle then pulled himself upright. The Kathirib roared around him, like the tossing wave of a forest under a raging gale, and charged.

Alaina jumped to her feet, yelling, knees braced against the rock, heedless, scop to a battle. The Twilkets answered the Kathirib, hundreds of voices welling in a shout.

Faisal spun Zahir away from the warrior and raced for the Twilket defense. At his back spread the Kathirib, horses and warriors speeding to catch him. The pounding of hooves and camel pads and savage yells gusted faintly around Alaina. No chance for the prince to show them Hala's letter, or time to set ink to parchment.

The Twilkets braced in their close-packed wall a bowshot from the base of the mountain protecting their backs. Tae yelled a deep-throated order. The first line lowered lances. Twilkets behind them lifted sword and shield.

The Kathirib shocked into the line. Horses and men screamed. Falling, rising, men staggered, swung, hacked, and thrust in a confused mass of bodies.

Faisal pressed forward on the right end of the line. Zahir reared, striking out with hoof and teeth as Tae had trained him. Faisal held his lance under his arm, spinning Zahir to knock a Kathirib from his camel, thrusting through another who swung a blade madly at his head, his mouth a dark hole, open in a howl Alaina did not hear. A second swordsman cut at Faisal's back.

The prince swung his shield around to deflect the blow. He pulled his lance free of the first man, whipped the shaft over Zahir's neck and thrust up under the Kathirib's sword-arm. He flicked him from his saddle, an almond from its shell.

Alaina's mouth curved. A blow worthy of the best staff wielder. A warrior in a corselet of silver under a streaming white kaffiyeh closed from the side at a gallop, deadly lance ready.

"Faisal!" Alaina screamed, her hands hot and damp as if she wielded her staff beside him. Faisal did not hear. He could not. She could not guard his side. Alaina shut her mouth on a sob. Her blood thundered in her ears, her body tense as gold wire drawn ready for the fire.

Zahir spun on his rear legs. Faisal met the lance with his shield, deflecting it. Then Twilkets surged around him. Dust and noise hid him. Alaina sagged against the rock.

Sheyk Gershem gave good account for his people, holding the middle, leading the strongest Twilket warriors in a wide-angled spearhead formation. He lifted his lance, his thawb glowing in the sun shafts streaming through the clouds. The Twilkets gained a lance-length forward. And another.

Men fell or were unhorsed. The ends of the Twilket line shortened. Then shortened again as fighters drew in to cover each other.

Warriors fell close around Hafiz. Those left standing worked about a downed, thrashing camel. Hafiz gave good account of himself, for one who had foolishly pulled the sentries back. The Kathirib would have surprised them completely, but for Tae's insistence on scouting forays. The middle of the defense held then pushed ahead. Gershem's blade flashed in and out.

Faisal appeared through the dust, his brothers on either side of him guarding his back. "Bless you, bless you," Alaina whispered, her fingers digging into her palms. Etain nudged her shoulder with a whicker.

Alaina frowned, straining to see through dust and lowering storm cloud. On the Kathirib side of the plain, the wazir's man with the pale hair raised his weapon, as if he urged on the fight by his will alone. Far to his rear, camels drummed among the dunes. Many warriors in red and black appeared under a standard of the same. They formed up behind him. Another group on foot streamed from a shallow wadi to form up on his flanks. And then she knew.

Not a simple warrior, but an askar and one of the wazir's captains. The Baghdad askars stood in ranks around him, in Sirius Abdasir's red and black. One handed the captain a gold turban.

A few salukis ran among them. Alaina stared. The wazir dared his own daughter's life, sending his askars against them?

No. She did not believe it. Not after he had sent Kyrin across the sea to find Hala. There was greater treachery here than the Kathirib's broken oath. Alaina reached up to Etain's neck, clutched the mare's tasseled cheek-piece. If someone could speak to the captain . . . but he had given Faisal no chance.

Up and down the Twilket line, warriors struggled, parted, reformed. A dust trail billowed behind their ranks—Tae's galloping horse. A lull in the wind carried his voice. "Hafiz!" Tae bellowed as he passed, "Hold them!"

Hafiz, in a pure white thawb save where blood and dirt streaked his shoulder, raised his sword in acknowledgement.

The pale-haired askar raised his lance three times, and rode forward. His men followed, on foot and camel back. First at a camel's walk, then a trot, and finally a gallop. Lances flashed. Red and black and gold rippled. The less disciplined Kathirib had cleared the way.

Now all the Twilket lines were engaged, and far too short. They would be flanked in moments by the askars' charge. How such perfidy came to be would not change their fate.

Alaina's quill broke. Dumb, she dropped the feather, staring at her fingers. Thick and slow, they belonged to another. But her cold fingers missed something.

Riding in close formation, from each end of the ridge burst shrieking Twilkets on horses. Alaina jerked about in hope. Etain reared, brought back to earth by her hand on the rope. The warriors slammed into the second wave of askars and Kathirib.

Camels yawled, careening into other Kathirib, and split the enemy into three thrusting points of attack. Riders surged ahead, in furious conflict. Warriors ran behind. There were two enemies to every Twilket.

The red-robed askar drove toward Hafiz, sword out. Hafiz held the left side of the defense, slightly behind Gershem, while Faisal and his men desperately beat back a horde, two full prongs of the attack. The line to his right gave and collapsed inward.

Then Tae was there, sword in one hand, stick in the other. Men fell before the blur of his weapons, wheat to the reaper. Faisal's line reformed raggedly beneath the grey sky. The enemy was beaten back a few paces.

But the pale-haired askar spurred his horse, sword rising and falling as if with a life of its own, driving the Kathirib and his askars straight for Gershem. Hafiz swung his weapon to call his warriors to close up, his thawb dust-streaked. His men rallied. But there were fifty Baghdad warriors to their twenty, and Bedouin were used to swift attack and retreat on horseback, not to Tae's orderly reliance of every man on his brother's shield.

A dark shelf of cloud gathered in the southwest. There a winged shape dipped and hovered before the storm's edge in the last of the sun. Truthseeker.

A wall of roiling snow whirled below the clouds behind her. Alaina shivered at the bite of wind that reached across the plain. Farook had loosed her.

The askars' captain swung his sword around his head. His cry was lost in a din of pain and triumph. Men locked with each other, beasts wandered, rider-less. Warriors ran to and fro from knots of battle. Screams, cries, yells—the air shuddered with them. Alaina bit her tongue.

Warriors fell. Others fled before the pale askar. Hafiz's line was dissolving. Many would die. Snow would soon cover the battlefield in silent white. There was no one else. The confusion below was complete.

Alaina gripped Etain's mane and saddle—and paused. If she stayed as Faisal ordered, Hafiz would fall. He would never challenge or betray her or her prince again. She rested her forehead against Etain's flank with a wordless groan. Dark pits of choice opened.

She hated blood. And her own thought, that she would leave Hafiz to die; for advantage, for fear, for a path that led in old, sure ways to Kyrin and safety. She stared down over the rock. Surely the sheyk or Tae would stop the Baghdad warriors.

Below her, the archers Tae had posted moved toward the mountain's foot—shadowy shapes flitting from rock to tree to tamarisk. There were not enough.

The Twilket line would not hold. If she did not try, and Hafiz fell, her people would be surrounded. Down there, screams would ring in her ears. She would spill blood. Or more likely, die in a puddle of her own before she reached the man in red. Who was she—a scribe, not yet a prince's wife—to ride down the hillside and raise her staff to stop a tide of blood? Alaina's teeth chattered; her face was wet. Whether Hafiz and his warriors wanted her or not, they were her people.

Shivering, Alaina pulled off her hattah and cast it away. If she was going, if this was the end, she would give them something to stare at. Alaina withdrew Tae's hair pins and tucked them in her sash, careful of the points. If she had to use those it would be close work. A shudder shook her. Her hair tumbled around her shoulders. Cold snowflakes rushed to meet her on the air, tugging at the red-gold as she loosed Etain and mounted. She drew her staff from its thongs, dragged her sleeve across her face, and pointed Etain's head toward the plain.

The path she had picked for descent after the battle ran in a rough zigzag, often in the open. She rode it in jolting leaps and sliding turns. Gripping the mare with hands and knees, she could not stop shivering. Kyrin would tell her to go on. Another leap and shuddering jolt. Her face felt stiff, her cheeks frozen in the stinging wind. Why hadn't she learned to use a sword? Etain raced downward, steady and strong.

Alaina smelled rosewater, and the stink of battle. She could never go back. *Master, Father, give me strength.* Men fell just below them. *Kyrin, I love you.* She gripped Etain as she lunged for the last slope. At the heavy landing Alaina's teeth slammed together. *Faisal, my heart . . .*

Two Twilkets striving to hold the line parted in the howling melee. A Kathirib lancer swung his mount between them, a battle grin on his bearded face as he chose which to kill.

Alaina kicked Etain at him. He tried to take off the mare's head with his blade. Etain twisted aside, near unseating Alaina. She swung her staff hard. It connected with the warrior's temple then his saddle was empty. Another man yelled at her and lifted a lance. She batted it aside and cracked her staff against his knee, then thrust at his stomach and throat. He reeled back and away.

She cringed at a whistling noise behind her and lifted her staff over her head. A heavy strike from her flank sliced toward her lower hand. Etain spun to face the threat at her rear. Alaina slid her hand back to her waist and yielded to her attacker's strength. The warrior's blow glanced down. She redirected his blow to the end of her staff whirring over her head. Then struck where his thick neck met wide shoulders. His collarbone snapped like a twig. His sword faltered. She left him and surged forward. There was someone she must find.

A falcon cried shrilly. Warriors fell away from her. Truthseeker plunged from the sky.

Alaina brought her arm up, warding her face. Truthseeker's landing near clouted her from the saddle. Alaina grasped Etain's mane, pulled herself up, and lifted the flapping falcon. The hand on her staff was leaden, her arm under Truthseeker burned.

There. Hafiz—and an askar robed in red, their mounts shoving for position. She was through the line.

The askar's pale hair was matted with sweat. His gold turban had disappeared. His blade darted for Hafiz's side. Without Alaina's conscious thought, Etain leapt, and halted. The captain cut at Hafiz again, blade hitting lance with a dull sound. Cornstraw hair and brows darkened by sun, flattened over a generous mouth set with effort. A face she knew.

"Seliam?" Alaina choked. His head turned. Hafiz stabbed at him with the end of his broken lance. Seliam twisted in his saddle, caught the shaft and followed it hand over hand toward Hafiz. Hafiz's eyes widened and he yanked against his attacker's pull. Seliam let go, and Hafiz fell backward, clutching vainly at his saddle.

Alaina nudged Etain, who sprang sideways. Truthseeker mantled for balance. They faced the captain. Behind them Hafiz screamed, "Not you!" His voice seemed far away.

Seliam sat quiet on his chestnut. He leaned forward, as if they spoke at a scribe's table together. "You shelter my lawful prey."

Truthseeker spread her wings. Alaina did not move.

In her old master's house Seliam once fought her sister to settle a wager. If he had won, Kyrin would have been a cripple, and she herself his wife by force. By the word of Sirius Abdasir, wazir to the caliph. His captain wore red then. Like master, like dog.

Still a betrayer, despite her message. What had Faisal said? 'Do not judge him too harshly. He is torn between debt of blood and debt of word—between your sister who held his life and his master who holds his oath—and now you, who hold his friendship.' Her lip curled. "Your lawful prey? You are a traitor to us all!" Seliam's men slowed behind him. There was no time. Alaina bit her lip.

"Move!" Seliam shouted. Alaina gathered herself. He raised his blade. "For the most excellent wazir!" The chestnut leaped, and crashed into Etain.

With a scream, Truthseeker launched straight for a red-black figure beyond Seliam, outstretched talons seeking his face. Alaina leaned away from the rush of her wings. She locked her legs to stay in the saddle, and the blur of Seliam's blade slipped past her face. His lips pressed together, bloodless.

Her staff took him in the side of the head. His eyes rolled up and he slumped over his horse's neck. Then the archers were shooting, and more men fell.

Faisal shouted, "Yield to the caliph's seal! It is his word of peace!"

A Baghdad askar yelled back at Faisal, who reined Zahir up beside Sheyk Gershem. Hala's letter fluttered in the prince's hand, its seal bright. The warrior stared at it a moment, and then jerked toward Alaina. His eyes widened as he watched Seliam crash to the ground.

Carefully, the askar sheathed his blade and lifted empty hands. Up and down the field, weapons dropped, Baghdad askar and Kathirib alike .

Alaina felt cold from the inside out. She slid from Etain, and found Seliam had not missed completely. The cut above her knee was raw torture. Blood blackened her blue trousers. But it was a small thing.

Seliam's chest rose and fell. She went to him. Her leg weakened under her, and she thudded to her knees.

His eyes opened. "How—" Then his back arched and he gasped for air, limbs quivering. Alaina touched his shoulder, feather-light, her eyes burning. The blow she landed could not possibly do this, though she had aimed to crush his throat. In a fight for her life she could not do otherwise.

Restlessly he turned his head. The back of it was wet, his hair stuck to his skull like darkened corn silk. The rock beneath was a spike.

Her breath caught. "Why?" she cried. "You didn't have to! Why didn't you heed my message?"

His fumbling hand sought hers. "My master must—" he choked. "Ware the asp." His voice trailed away. His tight grip eased.

Hafiz grabbed Alaina's shoulder, his dagger naked in his hand, his fixed grin on Seliam. His eyes were bloodshot, his kaffiyeh gone, his face streaked with dirt and blood, nose swollen. He shoved her aside.

"No!" Alaina cried, rage and sorrow held in by a thread. She released Seliam's limp fingers and yanked at Hafiz's arm. "His spirit is gone." Hot tears rushed down her face. Had Seliam meant to miss her throat with his first blow?

Why had he done it? Ware the asp? What did that mean? Now his blood had been spilled, along with some of hers. Alaina's breath stopped. Blood. Her trembling hand found her wound. She drew her palm across the wet cloth and open flesh. Then slowly she stretched her bloody hand above Seliam's face.

And stared into Hafiz's hard eyes. "I took this askar's life for you. By my blood shed in your defense this hour, your Nur-ed-Dam against my sister and my father is sated." Her voice rasped.

Hafiz caught her arm in a grip of iron. Alaina held his gaze and did not resist. A warrior behind them called something she could not distinguish. Hafiz released her.

It would please Seliam, the askar she knew, that he repaid Kyrin so well in the end. Nothing must stop her taking the gift he gave. She drew her wet fingers across her brow and cheek. "Blood erased by the blood shed." She lifted Seliam's sword from his outstretched hand and slid her palm gently along the blade. "Forgive me," she whispered. She bowed her head then lifted the weapon and turned. "By the blade and the blood, your worth to lead is proven. Sheyk Hafiz, I beg you, take it."

"You would give me this?" His hand closed slowly on the sword.

Her wound burned. "It is a scop's place to tell the stories of her people. This day it is your honor to shape your own. Shall this be your victory, or shall it belong to a Nasrany?" She left him his pride, and did not say a woman.

Staring at her, he nodded, short and sharp. "I will take the victory. If the prince does not seek my place." It was grudging warning.

"Burn it—"

"Burn what?" He stared at her darkly, fingers tightening about the blade.

Best she say what she meant, and burn nothing more. Alaina swallowed hard. "Forgive my foolish words. I wish peace, as does my prince." *Leave us.* She glanced at the sword a last time.

He grinned then, the corner of his mouth turning up, like a smug child who has won a coveted sweet by misbehavior. He bowed slightly and turned away.

Alaina slumped. Triumph felt far from her. She was strong. That truth was a fearful thing.

Snowflakes melted into Seliam's sightless gaze. Life, gone. There was no trace of ashy gold about him now. She pulled his black sash free to cover his eyes, her arm hot with pain. Truthseeker's talons had been sharp, and she'd had no glove.

A small round case fell from the black silk and tinked to the gravel, fast disappearing under white. Alaina opened the message case. She held up a bit of fine paper, and blinked her sight clear.

I do not ask Thee to take them out of the world, but to keep them from the evil one. They are not of the world, even as I am not of the world. Sanctify them in the truth; Thy word is truth.

It was a part of John's letter she'd scribed in Ali's house long ago, which Kyrin had given to Seliam when they parted, when she could have taken his life, and did not. Alaina put the paper back and laid it in Seliam's hand, then curled his fingers about the case on his chest. That he carried it gave her hope. He might be at peace with the Master of the Stars despite his treachery. He said he had committed none. But someone had.

His words had been strange. Ware the asp. Who was the asp? She was trembling. Where was Truthseeker?

"Alaina!" Faisal dropped from Zahir and ran toward her. He fell to his knees and crushed her to him. His sword hilt dug into her ribs. She slid her hands about his neck and kissed him. She cared not who saw. His knee touched her leg, and she cried out. He shifted back, his fingers cupping her bloody face. "You're hurt!"

She shoved away his anxious touch in irritation, pain growing. "There is treachery about. No, I'm not wound–witless, Faisal. Listen."

She closed her eyes the better to see the words. "Seliam said to ware the asp—" She paused for a breath and found herself looking at grey sky. Her prince loomed above her, pulling up her sleeve, his eyes full of her hurts. She whispered, "He could have killed me, could have tried harder. He said Hafiz—was his lawful prey. Why did he think it lawful?" She should say more about Hafiz. Her tongue was too thick. "His master must do something."

There was a frown on Faisal's face, but darkness blotted out the falling snow and swallowed him.

12

Strength and honor are her clothing. ~ Proverbs 31:25

Tae sighed, glancing at Alaina. Faisal had carried her to the bottom of the mountain then lifted her carefully up to Tae's saddle. She had not awoken during the ride, when he carried her to her bed, or when he dressed the talon punctures in her forearm and the sword cut on her leg. She had been through much, and done much.

Busy with warm milk and dates for the wounded, Hafiz's wife hovered near the door with a jug and bowl. She cleared her throat pointedly, her eyes gimlets of suspicion, aimed at any male in Alaina's tent. Tae glared at her. Basimah could wait.

He'd bound Alaina's leg while dictating a letter to Farook, which Kentar was even now speeding to Sirius Abdasir. The wazir must know someone had written a letter of war to the Kathirib and his own askars and sealed it with his seal. Seliam's first warrior had shown the letter to him after the battle. Tae pursed his lips. He himself would follow Kentar and both letters to Ali's house when he could. Prince Faisal should not be risked.

Tae's mouth quirked. The prince hovered outside, barred from Alaina's side by Basimah. Alaina stirred on her bed, and

Tae laid his hand on her forehead. She was not fevered. It was good. Farook had given him a third letter.

He sighed. Would that it had come at any time but now.

Tae-shin, first among Hwarang, first in my heart. My honored husband, my father gives me leave to speak at last as the red leaves fall. Is it not enough? Our son has seen five seasons without his father. The venerable Kuksun Paekche Kim has declared it so.

Our little Ryung-suk has been my bright rock. Come back to us, my husband. In obedience, Huen.

Love for him and anger at her father underlay Huen's words. His son, Ryung-suk. Tae's fist knotted. Paekche had concealed the boy from him. He must go back and take them away from his father-in-law. But it had been so long. Was there a seed of anger in Huen's heart for him also? He rubbed his face with his hand. He had grown used to exile—even throve in it, by the grace of the Master of the Stars.

Where would he find a place for Huen where neighbor women spoke kindly and boys laughed and men would be honored to learn Subak beside him? He would search up and down his land, and begin his house elsewhere. But not yet.

I must finish this thing so Ryung-suk may look up to his father. Paekche will not hide behind my Huen, he will not conceal his darkness in her pure heart and hand.

He had dictated in a voice of stone to Farook, and his scribe's hand had trembled.

My heart aches, my Huen. Paekche's seal that sent me from you must be the seal that restores. Tell our Ryung-suk his father has something he must do, but he hopes to return in a season. Nothing but my oath could keep me from you. Daughters of your heart and mine, not of blood, are threatened. Lift us to the Master of the Stars, keeper of my heart. He has kept me thus far—I believe he will keep me unto your side. I wait to hold you both.

Tae-shin, or Tae Chisun. So I am now known.

Paekche did not know what he had unleashed. Tae leaned down and kissed Alaina's forehead. For now, he had an anxious prince to soothe, treachery to search out, and a wedding to oversee. It would be good to see her safe.

Her indrawn breath warned him, and he drew back. Alaina whimpered. In the light of the lamp, her eyes were large with poppy for the pain. Then she curled up on her side and sobbed.

Tae gathered her close, murmuring, "You did well. Alaina, you have wielded your weapons well. Let Seliam go." If he had learned one thing from exile, it was that his daughters needed his arms around them. As did his Huen, and his son. Their time would come. His tears fell on Alaina's head.

§

Alaina touched the tight bandage on her arm, tugged at it, sighed, and bent over the table. After three hands of days the arm was sore and itched like fury, but was well enough. Stretched straight under the scribe table, her leg still ached. The morning sun warmed her back, passing under the side of the tent she had raised.

Under her hands, pale paper blazed in the light like Seliam's hair. Alaina shook her head. It was hard to order her mind to her task. But it was high time to begin her entry of the battle for the Chronicle, to write away the pain and the horror—and also to set down the courage and the lives gained. In time, she would feel the joy of what they had won.

Hala and her father, the wazir, had come with many old friends from Ali's house for the wedding. Their voices rose and fell among the tents. She could not face them yet.

Would they see a woman who reputedly killed with the death touch, or merely the wife of their prince? Or would they see a weary scribe, a healer who could not go back on her choice? Who knew that even if she could, her heart must choose the same?

Alaina brushed her chin with Faisal's red quill. A ball of warmth nestled on each side on her. While Cicero and Sahar hunted, the pups stayed, for they did not yet have the strength, wind, or muscles to pursue the reem. Many gazelle and hares were needed for the wedding feast, to say nothing of camels and sheep. But the pups were a tether to truth in the moments her mind and emotion fought each other. The truth of the power and goodness of the Master of the Stars, who worked within all things, despite evil. Alaina smiled. Gwenich lay at her left hip.

Her moonlight pale coat held a dusting of red from her brows to her tail. The pup's strong legs and oversized paws, now twitching in desert dreams, had hinted early at swift coursing. More telling to Alaina, when Gwenich considered which sibling it was most expedient to leap on from ambush among the cushions, she picked neither the weakest nor the strongest. Gwenich thought more than the rest. She was also first among her litter mates to growl at threat, standing her ground before Alaina on wide-splayed legs when she was barely able to walk. When Alaina picked her up, her tongue was warm, she smelled of milk, and her honey-gaze laughed, her tail thumping Alaina's wrist.

At near four moons, the pup would be of an age for short hunts soon. The saluki opened her mouth in a yawn then sniffed, and gently pricked Alaina's hand with growing, needle teeth. Kyrin would be pleased.

Alaina stroked Gwenich's soft head again and flipped the pale ears with a finger, though a lump grew in her throat. Gwenich did not now need protecting. As she did not. She had killed, and she could not go back.

"I thought I would find you here." Faisal stood before the doorpost, his arms crossed, the length of the scribe-table between them. His brown silk thawb glowed and his white turban brought out the rich brown of his gaze. Unsmiling, he studied her.

Why did her heart pound as if she faced the Kathirib? Rather breathless, Alaina blurted, "Tae said you were hunting."

"They have no need of my lance. Truthseeker will blind the reem with her swift dives, and Hafiz's saluki will bring them to ground as well as Ciero or Sahar." He shrugged and lowered his voice. "Many speak well of Hafiz—since my brothers saw him fight the wazir's war leader." Faisal stared at her. "There are differing accounts of how the askar fell."

Alaina rolled Gwenich on her back, extricating her hand from her jaws, ignoring her mock-growl. "I know Hafiz carries Seliam's sword." She did not look at him.

Faisal crossed the rug, knelt, and gripped her shoulders. "He fell under *your* staff, Alaina."

"Yes. And I chose to end Hafiz's Nur-ed-Dam. I chose that. I would not have him hurt any of us more than he has."

Faisal shut his eyes with a look of pain, then dropped his hands and rose to pace back and forth. "They should know the truth! Alaina, you will be my wife." He turned to her. "Hafiz is not your match, nor mine. My brothers should know who took the victory. It was not Hafiz."

Alaina cocked her head. "It angers you, to leave without their honor. I am sorry that he wounds you, that Hafiz draws their hearts, their tongues, their love."

"No!" Then her prince sighed. "Yes, that is true, but it is more than that." He shook his head again and glared at a spot of sun on the rug. "They should know your worth."

"As they know yours—through me." The bitterness of it choked Alaina. "It will always be so, since the death touch is revealed. They will call it that, whisper of the touch of death, though I did not use it." Gwenich rolled upright and yipped, tipping her head to the side, inquiring what was the matter. Alaina sat back with a frown. "I fought Seliam because I did not want your people, *our* people, to fall. I gave Hafiz the sword."

"You gave it?" The words were strangled and quiet.

She clenched her hands, the slender quill hard against her palm. She had chosen. "Was it not a good trade, that he would leave us in peace and know we are no threat?"

"Though I challenge him not, he walks and talks as if I have no further interest in my people. They are yet my blood." He came close and looked down at her, his mouth drawn and hard with pain, a pain that gnawed at her.

"Faisal, I would not have him hurt you. I care not what he thinks of me."

"You ought to care more what *they* think, the men and their wives, our people. Why did you leave the mountain? You were to chronicle the battle. You might have died." His voice rose.

She frowned. "What troubles you?"

He did not answer, merely huffed out a breath and shook his head.

Alaina swallowed. "Yes, I might have died. But it seemed certain many of you *would* die, and all come to death in the end. My life is bound up with you, with them." She waved her hand, indicating the tents without, and her mouth quirked. "Though Basimah thinks me unsuited for this land, they know I was as untimely born from the beginning. What I do will not change their thoughts so quickly." Alaina sobered. "I could not stand by—and watch, though sometimes I wish I could have."

He shook his head, hard. "If I had only held the line—"

"It was not you, but Hafiz who gave way."

"No, I ought to have held it. That was my place. Tae would have helped, and you would not bear these wounds now." His mouth flattened.

"Even a prince cannot be all things to all of us, Faisal. You cannot be everywhere. You are no Djinn, and I am thankful for it." He did not laugh as she meant him to, only glanced at her. Spreading her hands, she went on, "Is it not good that Hafiz holds his place as heir in Gershem's eyes? And you have chosen another path? The Master of the Stars guides us." She reached up and touched his arm. "What ill thought holds you, my prince?"

Faisal laid his hand over hers and looked down at their joined fingers in the sunlight. With a wry twist to his mouth, he said softly, "I fear jealousy has clawed me. You did well—but for giving yourself to the Kathirib blades." He touched her cheek. "My beautiful Alaina."

Jealousy? She drew back, her voice sharp. "And who else should I put before their blades?"

He sobered. "That is my place."

"And my place is to let you? This may be a selfish thought, but do not ask me to let you or anyone else die without doing what I can." She glanced at Gwenich, then with a softer look at him said, "Even our noble ones know *that* is owed, my prince."

"Will you not listen?"

Alaina laid her quill on the table and tucked her hands under her arms. She did not understand, and a chill crept in. "What would you have, my lord?" She had only defended those of his blood.

Faisal swallowed hard. Abruptly, he knelt to face her, reaching. "My place is to guard your life, and I would have you guard it, for it is also mine. As it is your peoples'. When you speak, you must consider—that Hafiz, he—"

"That my word to Hafiz is *your* word? Is that your meaning?" If that was the thorn in his heart, he must know it was not so. He was a man in his own right. Surely he must not think so. "That could never be true. You are the prince." Could he not see that?

Fire grew in him to match the heat in her. He drew back, and banked the coals in his gaze. "I think our hearts must teach us what each must do. You have been but a short time with us." His stiff words fell like stones.

Alaina closed her eyes. Why had she pressed him so? "If we do not speak of what pricks us, how will we know our hearts, and more, the will of the Master of the Stars?" She paused. "I do not understand your thought."

"No." He hesitated then turned away.

"Please, tell me. What is it about Hafiz, Faisal?"

He turned, flinging out his hand in negation. "It is not him, jackal though he is!"

"What then?"

"I, I know not, if you cannot see it—"

She pushed herself up, dragging her leg from under the table. He put a hand under her arm and steadied her briefly. With an injured look, Gwenich stalked away. The other pup's ears pricked, and he pounced on her. They wrestled, and thumped into Alaina's ankle. Pain flared. With an excited yip, the pups tumbled out of the tent.

She muttered, "I'll surely give your people something to laugh at if I cannot walk to my own handfasting. I'm likely to fall on my nose before Hafiz and his wife." Maybe her prince felt the same, unsure of himself, and of her.

She stared up at him, twisting her fingers together so she would not grip his arm in appeal, as Basimah would say, with womanly wiles. She did not wish to sway him that way. "I would not shame you, before Hafiz or any other."

"I speak nothing of your shaming me." Faisal captured her arm gently again. She rather thought he sensed what she felt

when they touched. "It is only that I fear for you. I ought to protect you. I did so ill, and I sorrow for it."

Alaina stared in wonder. "You did no ill. It was my will to
fight."

"Yes." He grimaced. "So they say."

"*What* do they say?"

"That you—you carry the lance. And I, the quill." His eyes
found hers, hot with shame. "Their words are of no worth."

"They hurt you, so their words have meaning, do they not?"
she said softly. Her mouth flattened. "We will change that meaning." It would not be easy. "Burn it." This time, it fit.

Stepping toward the door, she tripped over a cushion and
clutched at the tent pole. She pulled something loose. The side
of the tent shivered down, enclosing them in dim stuffiness.
Alaina laughed and hefted the pole. The arm hurt, but it obeyed.
"Get your lance."

"What?" He turned her to face him, his hands warm on her
shoulders in the dimness.

"What I said." She pushed back her laughter that threatened
to turn to tears of pain. "Best to settle this before we give our
oaths to each other."

"Alaina? That leg has drained the blood from your head. You
want to spar *now?*"

She laughed in truth. "Please, Faisal, I know what I'm about."

"Do you say so?" He shook his head and sighed, then swung
out under the side of the tent, his mouth twitching. Was that a
frown or amusement? She hoped he would not bring Tae back
with him, or Basimah. Then she would have to argue with them.
Though it might be better so, to have witnesses rather than her
and Faisal's word alone.

The leg twinged. Alaina rubbed it. It would not thank her for this. She worked to raise the side of the tent again, though without its pole, which she kept beside her, it sagged.

Faisal returned with his lance and her staff. "That pole is unwieldy. I will not take unfair advantage." He threw the staff to her, and she dropped the tent pole, kicking it behind her. Her right leg withstood her weight, though it protested with fire.

"Well then." She took position across the table from him. "Now you will be as hobbled as I." She lifted her chin, defiant. "We start on even ground. None can say my leg will matter, each of us bound to stay within an armspan of the table."

"You mean to do this." It was his turn to wonder. "Would it not be better to let Hala take the pain from your wound with Tae's salve and rest? It is near time for your henna painting! "

She smiled, a sweet smile. "Let the loser be the first to touch the earth in an uncontrolled fall. Hala and the henna will wait for our learning."

Her prince said something under his breath that included Basimah, and lifted his lance in a slow arc.

"Will it be a handful of moments before Hafiz's wife comes, or only one?" Alaina cocked her head at him and smiled.

Faisal pressed his mouth into a line and made a cautious jab. She leaned aside and avoided it without raising her staff. Tae had been training him. "Do you not have more than that, my prince?"

Exasperated, he shot her a look. She rapped him a blow on the head, and fire came up in his eyes. Noting her satisfaction, he nodded grimly and reached behind him to the shelf for a block of wood she used to grind ink—and capped his lance tip. Alaina braced her feet.

The first rattling fury of wood against wood drew Farook at a run. Neither she nor Faisal saw fit to answer his open mouth as he gaped at their battle. Sweat had started on Faisal's face. Alaina felt the same crawling down her back.

She batted aside his thrust across the low table. He withdrew his weapon, feet solid, and tested her guard up one side and down the other. She caught every blow, rapping him sharply in return on the top of the head, on his shoulder, on his side. He grimaced and gave before her blows.

After Farook, Tae came. He crossed his arms and rocked back on his heels, grinning inside the doorway. The wazir stepped inside, Greek features quizzical beneath his high brow. A crowd was gathering.

With a grunt, Alaina stepped away from Faisal's smashing blow. She slid her staff between his lance and her side. The rich green of Sirius's thawb remind her of another fight, one to deceive him. The wazir inclined his head with a smile. His golden skin had lightened, hidden from the sun of late, as if he now warred more often in palaces of stone. He motioned for Farook to open every side of the tent.

Burn it! She could use the light, but why did the wazir reveal her contest with the prince for all to see? She ducked a blow and gave one. Did the wazir seek division among the Twilkets? Or did he understand her thought and approve? Always, Sirius Abdasir pursued advantage.

Farook leaped to obey, beating Hafiz's young followers to the first pole. Loyal Farook. Alaina's mouth turned up.

A glancing blow stung her ear. Wool-gatherer, to lose sight of Faisal and his weapon! She shook her head and shrugged away the pain. His blunted lance bit her knuckles, headed for her side again. With a gasp, Alaina twisted away, almost losing her grip on her staff. She fended Faisal's swift jab at her face and his sweep toward her knees, and dealt another blow to his side.

Their watchers applauded. Some cheered her, and some the prince. Hala's lips were parted and her eyes shone. Nimah flapped her aba in encouragement. Beside Mey and the close-gathered women, Basimah raised her hands in horror, her voice shrill. Sheyk Gershem appeared at Tae's elbow, stroking his beard. More Twilket hunters spread around them. Hafiz held a hooded Truthseeker on his arm, for once without expression.

The moment for change had come. She turned to Faisal. "So, what do they say, Twilket prince?"

Red flooded Faisal's face at Hafiz's unpleasant chuckle. But the prince mastered himself, and his attack did not falter or haste. He scored a hit on her, and another.

Alaina did not allow herself to wince. If that lance tip were unwarded she would be using one arm and hobbling. Her leg was pure fire.

The finish was in sight. There. Catch the wood, twist so—his lance flew from his hand. She leaned on her staff, panting. "Is it proven?"

He took his weapon from Farook, who held it out to him, and faced her again, wordless. He raised it to guard. The quiet was deafening.

He was not giving in. Alaina sighed. And thrust straight and vicious for his stomach. He turned it with a blow of his lance butt. He learned even as they fought. Alaina's eyes stung with sweat but her smile widened.

He caught her hard on her bandaged leg. Alaina staggered, gritting her teeth, and the crowd drew a collective breath. *Direct the pain—loose the skill.* Her staff hummed forward and back. She struck for his temples, his side, his knees. Controlled, up, down, and around. It was everything she knew of the staff.

Faisal managed to protect his head, but he curled with a grunt when she thumped his side for the third time in a row.

He shifted his weight. She whirled her staff toward his thigh. It connected. He was going down, and he knew it as his jaw tightened and he threw all his strength into a blow against her staff. She met his vigor with increased speed. Her stave snapped, caught at the spot shaved by the Kathirib's sword.

Off balance, Faisal began to tumble forward, and turned it into a prodigious leap over the table. He crashed into Alaina, and the ground met her shoulders as she fell into a backward roll. She ended on top, lost one piece of her staff and struggled desperately with him for the other, dust in her mouth. They rolled over, and he yanked the end of wood from her and threw it. His weight pinned her to the ground, his chest heaving. Rocks dug into her back. The skin around his eyes was tight with the hot intent of battle. His breath came fast.

Instantly, Alaina struck at his temple. He caught her palm, bent her arm to the ground. She leaned up to his ear. "Good." It was half a groan of pain, and his breathing hitched.

"No," she said, on a sudden breathy laugh. And louder, "I yield! I could kill you here, but my leg hurts and you're on it. And please, leave me the gift of my arm. I need it to scribe."

He hurriedly drew his knee back from her leg, but kept a cautious hold on her arm. Alaina gathered her strength—and tried to throw him off with a wild heave. He instinctively slammed her to the earth.

She gave a grunt of pain which ended in a gasp for breath. In sudden doubt, his eyes closed and his mouth worked, his hands relaxing their hold.

"So I baited you, my prince—now they know *your* steel." Alaina coughed on the dust, and grinned. "You are a prince indeed. Not easily angered, not one to fall for tricks." She paused for air. "It is proven. If I had faced you in battle instead of Seliam, it would have ended differently. Men are more than twice my width of arm, therefore, my father gave me my staff to allot the touch of death. This day it availed nothing. I yield."

Incredulous, Faisal stared at her, his amber gaze wide, giving her his shock and joy. Then his chest shook with growing inner laughter. "Alaina, my Alaina," he whispered. "I would not again test that touch." His moment of surprise was clear to all, as was their respect for each other. He found her hattah and wound it about her hair. He helped her up, meeting the gazes of the men with a glare. Gershem grinned, and clapped him on the shoulder. Faisal flushed, but his head was high. Tae inclined his head gravely. The rest of the men murmured low words of approval.

Basimah stared at Faisal, her gaze hard. Alaina gave her a small, flickering smile. Basimah blinked. Alaina hoped Hafiz's wife would let go her ill will once she got over her amazement.

Truthseeker ruffled her feathers on Hafiz's arm. He moved through the hunters and held the falcon out to Faisal stiffly. The prince looked at the warrior a moment, then stepped close and raised his arm. Truthseeker sidled onto it, waggling her tail feathers, ruffling herself into peaceful order, head bobbing. "Did she hunt well?" Faisal's voice was steady.

"Yes . . ." the rest of Hafiz's words died beneath the sudden talk and laughter rising around the prince in a wave. Men touched his shoulders and arms in respect, inviting him to eat at their fires.

It was done. The wazir had gone. Did he find what he sought? Hala watched her, eyes narrow. Alaina wavered; her smile faded. Did Hala think her pleasure at her own defeat odd? She shifted a step. She must get off her leg. Sweat broke out on her face.

Hala and Mey rushed to her. Nimah wormed through the press with a wrinkled brow. Alaina let out a soundless breath. She was glad it was over. Her prince was proven. And Umar could not gloat, this time. As Kyrin said, the moment truly was vast.

13

Blood and Truth

Judge with truth and judgement for peace. ~ Zechariah 8:16

Tae grinned inwardly. Gershem's stare betrayed his interest. He was a wily old goat. The sheyk listened to the talk between the wazir's warriors and his own, searching for advantage around the fire, in the minds swirling with ill will, covered by smiles and smooth tongues. Tae was content. His enemies were under his eye.

Umar entered and strode to Sirius, touched his forehead to the earth, then stood to murmur in his ear. The wazir grinned and laid his hand on his shoulder. Every eye fastened on the wazir, who gestured outside in high triumph. "The caliph is just. Would you see his decree for your traitor?"

Everyone rose in a rustle of thawbs and sandals. Following at Tae's shoulder, Shahin, sheyk of the Aneza said in his ear, "Will the caliph's justice, blessed be he, favor the wedding of your prince?" His hawkish face was wary.

Tae said dryly, "As long as the peace may hold, sand to sand." Shahin grunted.

Tae ducked through the tent door and fell silent. Outside, a few salukis of Umar's Hand sniffed about a dusty heap at the wazir's feet, growling. A fly buzzed about the shredded leather sandals at one end, and the back of a dusty head at the other. From beneath the thawb thrown carelessly over the body, one wrinkled arm protruded. Sirius nudged the heap with his foot in disgust. With a sniffing snort, one saluki licked his reddened muzzle, shook his head, ears thwapping his skull, and trotted to the shade of the sheyk's tent. Sirius Abdasir looked after the beast then raised his gaze to the guarded stares of the warriors, his face like stone. The copper smell of blood filled the air.

"So falls Kaish of Jedda, who thought to mock the most excellent. This Kaish scribed a false message I did not dictate to the Kathirib, without the Caliph's authority, and set my seal to it. You are witnesses to justice, Sheyk Gershem, Sheyk Shahin, you and your elders." Sirius stretched out his arm to include Hafiz and Tae. "You have justice. Is it not so?"

"It is so. We witness it," cried many voices. Someone called, "Let him lie unburied for the jackals!"

Tae stared grimly down. *Beware the asp.* What was it he had heard? Prey never foresaw its doom before the asp struck. This time the Hand of Umar struck first.

Tae sought Gershem's eyes across the muttering ranks of Twilket and Aneza. The sheyk's old gaze was fierce. He was not entirely pleased. True salukis did not hunt men.

Umar said something low in Sirius's ear.

"Ah." The wazir beckoned to Tae. Tae bowed and stalked forward.

Umar took a sealed missive from his sash and laid it in Tae's hand, careful not to touch him. "Kaish had this in his possession." His wide-lipped mouth worked in his pale face. His eyes were cold.

Tae said nothing. The seal on the letter seemed whole, unbroken, the wax clear-formed. But one such as Kaish or Umar, even the wazir, knew several ways to make it seem so. It could even be rewritten, resealed. But he could not give any sign of suspicion. Tae broke the wax and read.

So. The hunt was afoot. "My thanks, this is welcome word." He said nothing more, folded the parchments and tucked them inside his thawb. It was a moment to test intents. Tae grinned, with expansive goodwill. "I must confer with my daughter, when Alaina is disposed to give an answer to her sister. She is to be wed under the next sun, by the caliph's favor, for her sister has greatly pleased the wazir. After they are wed, I go to my own land, to my wife and son." His gaze flicked from Gershem's keen interest, to Hafiz's bland attention. The wazir's mouth stiffened.

Tae turned his back. He sensed Sirius reaching for him, though he did not quite touch his arm. He stopped and inclined his head, waiting courteously.

The wazir's dark eyes bored into Tae's, his voice for his ears alone. "My Hala, the light of my eyes, spoke of your purpose to see Kyrin Cieri receive her writ of freedom in Britannia."

"My word on that yet stands, I assure you. I speak of after." Tae bowed.

"It is well." Sirius smiled slightly, considering him. "You are certain you will not return with me to the caliph, long may he live? The most excellent is a master with an open hand."

"I may teach in his court yet." Tae hesitated. "Many things are—unsettled—concerning my daughters." He kept his face clean of expression but for a courteous smile.

Hafiz glanced from Tae to Sirius.

The wazir frowned. "It would lighten my heart if you taught my master's askars. I have many men and beasts, gold and pearls, many lives under my hand. The caliph has more. A faithful man deserves his reward."

Tae inclined his head, silent. The wazir nodded and turned toward Gershem's tent.

Umar cleared his throat and spat expressively in the dust beside Kaish's head.

Tae glanced at him. The execution of the traitor was over before it began. One thread of the tale begun in Alaina's Chronicle was cut off. As the wazir's spy, Kaish had posed as an orange-seller when they arrived on the coast as captives, then in the midst of their escape he assisted Kyrin onto the wazir's ship to return to her father and seek Hamal. Was the old man's impact quite ended, his thread quite cut? How far did the poison of an asp reach? He had not seemed a completely dishonorable man. Tae took the wizened feet and said, with a curt jerk of his chin, "Let us take him beyond the tents. It is not fitting for him to lie here during our time of rejoicing."

Umar pulled the body from his grip. Tae balanced on instinct, waiting. Umar smiled, widely. "This one is not worthy of you. I will bear him." He flung the corpse over his shoulder as Tae watched. Kaish's head dangled at an odd angle. Salukis brought prey down from behind. The traitor should have wounds on his legs and back, possibly his arms or feet. Tae's eyes narrowed. Only his neck had been broken, and his throat torn out. He had been dead before Umar's unholy Hand of salukis got to him.

§

Alaina giggled. The lime-green henna powder Mey had ground, sifted, and mixed with lemon juice, tea tree oil, and honey the day before tickled her skin. With the tip of a quill, Mey drew the thick, rich dye mixture in careful lines along Alaina's foot. The feather had been removed from the quill to leave the hollow stem, and a pitch-proofed bag of silk hung on the end to feed in more henna mix when squeezed. Mey embodied the quick, gentle precision of the gazelle and its beauty, dark-eyed and small of bone.

Tea tree and rosewater from Alaina's bath sweetened the air. Her hair was soft, and she pulled the red gold through her fingers. Mey frowned at her toes in concentration. "Move not, if you wish to please the prince."

Alaina tried to smile. Sahar and her pups were banned, for young salukis chewed slippers, sniffed rosewater, or worse, lapped it, and had left paw prints on washed robes. She was more like Kyrin than she thought, if she could miss Cicero and the awkward, gangling flood of whipping tails and long legs, misplaced paws and all. Kyrin would hunt Gwenich well.

Alaina felt a true smile growing inside. She would see her sister soon, if nothing conspired to threaten the peace.

Mey wafted a long feather back and forth across the finished henna design, the air cool on Alaina's ankles. Was the feather from Truthseeker's wings? She leaned to look.

Mey pushed her back with a motherly smile. "Hala, the drying time is long. Will you read to us from Kyrin's letter?" Hala went to fetch it.

Alaina squinted at the delicate lines of paste that wound from her big toe, across the arch of her foot, and up her calf. The curling stems and life-like leaves reminded her of the vine with the white flowers that had graced Ali's wall in the women's court at his house. No one had ever told her its name. She remembered its sweet scent, white flowers, and green tendrils. To her people and to the Bedouin, white signified purity, and green was the color of life, riches, and abundance. She was no longer a slave, no longer hunted.

Nimah bent busily over the grass-green thawb Alaina would wear to handfast the prince of the Twilkets, adding a last thread of gold embroidery around the neck, a faint smile on her lips.

Alaina's smile faltered. If only her arms and legs did not have to be bound from nails to elbows, toes to knees until the sun rose. Then, when she had been unwound and the caked henna was gently washed away, the intricate body art, smoothed with oil and lavender, would lighten to a deep maroon. The blessing of henna.

"Now for your hands and arms. But don't move your feet." Mey plumped a cushion under Alaina's knees.

Alaina grinned suddenly. How would she eat with her fingers bound together like an Egyptian mummy's? "If I get hungry, will you bring me dates and milk?" she teased.

"Assuredly. With cakes and meat and fruit, too," Hala said as she stepped within the tent and unfolded Kyrin's much stained parchment with a dignified air. "Now, open your ears."

Alaina smiled and sank back against her cushions. She had read it before, delivered by Farook. But she would hear it again.

Umar shifted outside, where he could watch over the tent the wazir's daughter visited, his shadow swinging across the doorway. Alaina's brow furrowed. She was glad Farook also guarded them without. Opposite, Hala cleared her throat.

My dearest Alaina,

What do Tae and Shahin devise with Sheyk Gershem against the Kathirib? I did not think to start a war. Haply this missive will find Hala already with the excellent wazir. Not Hamal, but Hala. She comes to Araby as swiftly as sail can bear her.

Hala shot Alaina a grin and continued,

Sirius has his own honor and will keep his word. He will restrain his Hand.

I am glad you practice, sister. I will test your staff when next we meet. Do not think little of yourself even if for the moment your staff and quill are not needed. I will give you one of the wazir's blades for a copy of the Chronicle if you will craft one for me.

Your smile and encouraging heart are never to be lightly esteemed.

Mey's mouth quirked, and Alaina's neck heated. It might have been better to ask Hala to read a bit of her own verse. But then she would still insist on reading Kyrin's letter in return. Hala and the others thought it very funny that she had ever thought herself unneeded. They could not comprehend such a thing, though they readily admitted that skill with the staff and quill were unusual for a woman. Alaina sighed. She could endure the smiles. She had already started Kyrin's Chronicle.

Persevere as you said, and the reward will be greater than you dream—along with further tests—this is a training ground, after all. Remember, the Master of the Stars is generous beyond our deserts.

Enemies are hard to deal with. I hope the Twilket succession is clear. Peace is hard to grasp, and harder to keep. Faisal never was a thick stick.

No, he was not. Alaina smiled.

Give him greeting, and I hope soon to bless him as he has us. Do what you can for him, for my sake.

Alaina blushed. Kyrin would find it hard to believe her letter in reply. *She* found it hard to believe she was to have Faisal's warm arms, a place to give herself, to comfort, to strengthen, a safe place to love and be loved. To live their life with the Master of the Stars.

Dearest sister, you are yourself, and precious. The death touch—it is heavy. God will see you have it when you have need of it. You are closer to me than breath and bone.

Alaina touched her forehead with her fingers. The death touch was indeed heavy. But she had fought, and fought well. So Tae said, and he knew what he spoke of. She had defended her people, though not with the power of the scop. Her eyes stung. "So many died." It was a whisper.

Hala said gently, "My father's men and your Twilket brothers died without a lie in their mouths. Though it lay between them, it was not of their doing."

It was so. Alaina blinked. The Master of the Stars judged each for how they walked the path he set before them, not another's.

Her path was not finished, and seemed like to twist again. At least it did not twist toward the Caliph's court. She felt cold, imagining the use the wazir would find for her now.

Ahh, Alaina, I miss you. I so wish to see Cicero's pups. They will have been on their first hunt when this reaches you, will they not? I pray I may see you again.

Things are not all well, here. I would send a map—were there not danger of unfriendly eyes. One Lord Ludwin Mornoth did me and my friends much harm through his lackeys. Talik, a messenger of the strongholds, about my years, gave us much help. He moves well over stronghold walls, by the methods Tae taught us. Threats move in the shadows and do not show themselves. I will tell you more when I am free.

. . . when I am free. The wazir could not free her sister too soon.

Nimah glanced at Alaina. "Besides speaking of this Lord Mornoth, your sister thinks much of the one named Talik."

Alaina grinned. "I wish her all joy. But it is hard to tell where her heart leans. I will not say until I see her."

Mey smiled and impishly tickled Alaina's nose with the drying feather. "We know. It is better so. Kyrin will find her heart's desire, as you have."

I have a dear brother and a mother. My father is well—I cannot wait till you meet him! He and Tae have much to speak of: of defenses and the art of war, of the reach of those who trade across oceans. Hala is a friend, another sister. I pray you love her as I, for her heart is true, though wounded. I ask—do what you can.

Alaina blushed, and Hala shook with sly laughter. The vixen could laugh, remembering their first meeting and the threat of a certain lamp. There were not many words left to read. Alaina knew them by heart.

My thanks. Give Tae my greeting kiss, and I pray he has good news of Huen. Come to me as quickly as the excellent wazir's Hand allows, under the power of the Master of the Stars. I hold you in my heart.

Kyrin Cieri of Cierheld.

Because of their guards, Hala had not read Kyrin's first words. Alaina said them over silently.

Faisal Ben Salin's tents keep you well. You mentioned Umar. All men change, for evil or good—though often we cannot see it—above all, change in ourselves. Change is slow: thought on act, act on thought.

So it was. Because of Umar, because of their guards, she and the women would rest well this night.

Alaina wondered for the hundredth time what trouble Kyrin spoke of. Trouble among the strongholds, while she wed her prince. She frowned. She was not the Alaina who fled into the desert, despairing of advancement. That did not matter now.

Her prince was soon to be exiled. A man who loved her, who loved his people. Would he not go with her to help Kyrin, since he must go? A black stallion and some nine saluki noses would no doubt assist.

What had Nimah said about Zoltan putting henna on the salukis's noses before they hunted the desert? "Mey"—Alaina touched the Aneza woman's arm with her free hand—"will you get me a brush? I would put more henna on Cicero and Sahar and the pups. The sun should not burn them on the day of my gladness of heart. And might not Nimah and Hala paint my sigil and the prince's on their paws?" She had meant none other than herself to do it, but at the moment she could not move. It would while away the evening to watch the salukis. If they could be patient, so could she.

"Oh, please," Hala cried, "I would do so!"

"And I!" Nimah nodded firmly, "This way we will not add ill to your future."

Alaina's heart lightened. "No, and after I am unbound I will paint our sigil on your hands. From me to you. So you will join in our happiness!" She almost clapped, but Mey grabbed her wrists. "The henna!"

"Oh! I am sorry."

While Mey clicked her tongue and shook her head with a smile, Hala stood, clasping Kyrin's letter in her hands. With a twirl and a smile over her shoulder she said, "I will bear the weapons of the scribe and the warrior, beloved of the desert, in my henna!"

Mey released Alaina and stepped back, the henna etching bag in her hand. She raised her brows. "Shouldn't we offer this joy to Basimah and the rest of the women?"

"But I cannot paint them all! And you have only one henna quill. We would be up till the moon is high in the sky," Alaina protested.

"Ah. As for that, they would not miss this. They have their own henna, and they will come and paint each other. They will wear your sigil with pride, scop and she-lion of the Twilkets, chosen of our prince." Mey touched the back of Alaina's hand with her work-worn fingers and smiled. It was a stretch to call Faisal a prince of the Aneza. He and Kyrin once stayed but a short time with them, but Alaina knew what she meant. "Thank you," she whispered.

Hala leaned out the door. "Umar, be pleased to bring us the prince's saluki, and please call Basimah."

Alaina did not hear the rest. The women would come, and she could now tell them Tae had chosen well. For her own heart chose the same, the man Faisal Ben Salin. In the morn she would wed a prince of the sands.

14

Hearts Entwining

In Thy light we see light. ~ Psalms 36:9

Alaina shivered in the cool air. In a wide space between the black tents, she sat upon the scribe table, transformed into a wide, cushioned throne. Beside her, Faisal sank into the cushions, his weight threatening to draw her against him. She pushed down a giggle at his equally foolish smile, and leaned away. Handsome in red robes and a white turban, he had just one smudge near his ear. The henna she had painted on his hand had spread. He had not held as still as she.

The wedding guests sat in a half circle before their throne, Cicero and the pups ranged behind. All the waiting noses, human and saluki, sniffed hungrily at scents of cinnamon and honey, milk and raisins, almonds and dates; at hot roast lamb, gazelle, and pigeon piled on beds of fragrant, spiced rice.

Unhooded, Truthseeker mantled on Farook's arm. Drawing back her head, bold and beautiful, the falcon looked at all around her.

Alaina's mouth curved faintly. Though she had once thought she saw the tiger that haunted Kyrin, she *knew* what the falcon meant to her sister. And what the bird meant to her. She had feared the change falcons wrought in their fearless hearts, the power of irrevocable decision. But no more. She had made her own irrevocable decision, and was making another.

Faisal had promised to take her out after the ceremony to find a feast of truffles. They would camp in the sands, and he would show her how Sahar and Truthseeker hunted together. Sahar turned her head at some sound beyond the camp, intent, the henna on one paw and her nose barely visible against her bright coat. But it was just a noise. No enemy could break Tae's ring of watchers. And there were none left who would attack them, favored of the wazir.

Faisal moved his hand to cover Alaina's. On his brown skin the quill and lance crossed boldly, cradling an iris between. Alaina smiled at him as a hush fell over the crowd.

Sheyk Gershem strode out of his tent and Hafiz emerged from his. They moved solemnly to their places on either side of the throne. The old sheyk stood beside Alaina, and Hafiz, re-splendent in white, at Faisal's shoulder.

Tae glided through the circle of guests, holding before him a bunch of blue iris in his left hand, a silver cup steady in his right. He smiled at them in turn. Alaina's heart pounded. Faisal's damp palm trembled in hers.

Tae turned to speak to the guests. "We gather to witness my daughter and your prince as they join their lives this hour in sacred bonds. May their hands and hearts hold true in the light of the Master of all. Until they step into eternity." Then he knelt gravely on one knee and offered Faisal the cup.

Faisal took the silver vessel in both hands and held it out to Alaina. His eyes held heat and tenderness and a kind of awe. She lifted the cup and drank, not taking her eyes or her trust from him. Milk and honey with cardamom heated her tongue. He sipped after her. Then they stood and faced their people, lifted the cup toward the sky and the Master of the Stars, and drank again, each holding the cup for the other.

A great cheer shook the air.

Tae held up his arm, and the people fell silent, expectant. "My daughter holds my heart, as if she were blood of my blood. And this is my son, who has learned the true rights of power. I am proud. Their deeds are already great. Give them praise, and rejoice in their joy. So let it be." Tae laid the handful of iris, carefully wrapped in Gershem's dampened sash, in Alaina's hands.

She sank back onto the throne. The flowers' rich perfume rose around her. They were beautiful. Faisal's eyes were deep as he took them from her. He was beautiful, and brave and kind. She leaned forward and kissed him.

The people erupted in thunderous well wishes, and he froze, every muscle immobile. Alaina drew back, staring at the henna on her fingers. They were supposed to show little affection until in their tent. Burn it, why had she spoiled a perfect ceremony?

But then he was kissing her, and his mouth was fire. It could not be too soon to escape where they could be alone. She wanted to drink him in. At last Alaina pulled away, her cheeks hot. He grinned at her. She shrugged slightly, blushing again. A scop must get used to watchers.

She looked out over her people, laughing and cheering, their smiles undiminished by the wazir's stern-faced men, who upheld the gravity of the Caliph's askars. The wazir. Alaina hesitated.

With a wide smile, he approached, Umar impassive behind him. Hala followed, joyful tears in her eyes.

The wazir ceremonially kissed Faisal on both cheeks and turned to their witnesses. "These two are under the eye of the caliph. They enjoy his favor, as Tae Chisun has said." The wazir looked at Alaina, a glint of laughter in his dark eyes. "Long may you live, possessors of the twin jewels of wisdom and understanding. May they always give you the light to seek truth and justice."

Alaina bowed her head. What justice did he bid them seek besides Kyrin's freedom? Tae said the asp was dead. Unless the wazir meant them to seek justice for their people. Or themselves? But it was not the moment to speak or to question.

"And now, scop, the people wait for your words." The wazir gestured, inviting, no, commanding her. Alaina's stomach sank. She had not practiced for this!

Faisal urged her to her feet with his hand under her arm, his pride in her clear to all. Many faces gazed back at them. Alaina straightened under the weight of their regard. *Our life stories spring from our minds, our hearts, our spirits, under the hand of the Master of the Stars.*

Her voice came husky. "Life and death span your words and deeds. On these dawns of change I have known kindness among you, and some ill-will. Yet your courage to defend those you love lasts beyond the end of the sands. And you have come to love me, a Nasrany, who loves your prince. I thank you. Love that is tried fails not. The kind of love you have shown me is a root of joy."

Her heart warmed. "That is the last word of your scop! Now fill me with the good things I smell before I lose strength."

Laughing, Faisal pulled her to his side and assisted her down from their seat. All rose. Her prince kissed his sheyk on both cheeks, grinned at Tae, and pulled her toward the feasting platters. She was glad to leave behind the throne and all the eyes.

Umar trailed Hala nearby, guarding her. He caught Alaina's gaze and his hand twitched toward his scimitar. Did he remember throwing her staff to her on the dais in Ali's Blue Flower room? Umar's face twisted, and he turned from her. *Love ends not.* Did he resent the failure of his Hand? Alaina's smile fell away.

Beyond her prince, the wazir watched them narrowly, tugging at his beard. Alaina inclined her head soberly. Yes, she meant what she said, even for him who had chased her to the end of the earth. She would not hate the wazir or his Hand. Sirius crossed his arms. His guarded gaze gave her nothing.

Sheyk Gershem raised his arm. "Before we feast, who witnesses with me this bond before Allah?"

"I witness it." Hafiz signed the paper Gershem laid on the edge of the table.

"And I witness it before Jesu, the Master of all." Tae set his name below theirs.

"Ah, yes. There is that matter." Gershem looked at Tae slyly. "You owe the tax, being foreign, and Nasrany, and now of my house."

Hafiz grinned broadly.

Tae stiffened to stone and stared at Gershem. Then his shoulders relaxed. A smile played about his mouth. "It is a small price for peace between us, cheaper than blood. You no doubt wish to see your great-grandchildren."

"So I do." Gershem chuckled.

There were low comments among the men, and Basimah stared. Faisal's stomach grumbled. He shrugged, a little embarrassed, and Alaina cried, "Come, let us eat, or your prince will faint in sight of his table, before our journey!" He was even more their prince now, as he made ready to leave. She smiled up at him. "We need our strength."

There was a moment of silence. Around them lips twitched, someone chuckled, and then everyone roared. Alaina stared at them, and heat spread up her face. "I didn't mean—" Even the children joined in the glee. *Not again.* She was near tears when Faisal whirled her around. He kissed her and whispered in her ear, "What scop can give us such joy? You are good for us, my Alaina. You are the light of my eyes."

"If you say so." A smile crept over her face.

"I do." He kissed her again lightly, and she returned it, then everyone moved to the food.

Nimah walked along the line of platters spread on an expanse of rugs laid before Hafiz's tent. A flood of other women followed, hoping to secure a dish for the prince and his new wife.

Alaina's stomach growled, and her hands and legs quivered. She had not eaten this morn for fear of being sick. Now there was food and joy before her. "Faisal—"

"You also must pay the tax." Hafiz stood in their way, glancing from her to Faisal. The prince stiffened.

Hafiz smiled. "But it is my gift." He dropped the coins into Gershem's hand, touched Faisal's arm, and walked away.

Alaina watched him go in relief. He could have said, "It is my gift as your sheyk," but he did not. He and his wife meant them well—now that they were leaving. Alaina wrinkled her nose then laughed. As Kyrin would say, she was not the Master Scop, to weigh Hafiz's heart, and she was right glad of it.

The roast lamb, its skin crispy and speckled with herbs, beckoned her. And the rice, full of plump raisins. All the tastier, since she could share it with Faisal. Her Faisal, hers to love and hold. A prince, and a princess of the sands.

§

Her husband. Who knew that word could taste so sweet? All the sweeter after two hands of sunrises. They had wandered the sands and cooked their truffles while the sun sank into purple evening. They climbed the mountain where Youbib once took Truthseeker from an eyrie in the cliffs, and swam in secluded wadi pools in the cool first light. They laughed at the antics of

Cicero, Sahar, and their brood. And she held her breath in awe at their speed on the hunt and Truthseeker's adept, airy skill.

Alaina's brow wrinkled. She nudged Etain into a faster walk, though nothing could be dangerously wrong when Faisal rode beside her and their salukis paced down the trail ahead.

The pups' eager noses were busy. Truthseeker waited on her prince's arm for a rabbit or a reem to rise from their diligent hunt. Still, she did not trust—what? The quiet stillness was the hush before storm.

Was it Sirius Abdasir, who would soon sail to Britannia to honor Kyrin for redeeming Hala from her captors, who said he would give Kyrin's writ of freedom into her hand himself? But no wazir crossed an ocean to bestow honor on a former slave. Except to gain an end.

Did he trust Tae so much the more, now the asp was dead? Or hope to win his regard and the knowledge of the death touch with Kyrin's freedom? Mayhap he watched Tae as a threat. Did he think him a spy for his Land of the Morning Calm in the East, and seek to keep him close?

Alaina's forehead furrowed deeper. Or the wazir might seek the caliphate, with Tae at his back. Many men in red and black patrolled the caravan roads. But Tae would not betray those to whom he gave his word. Sirius had learned so. What if his allies fought each other? Which would Tae Chisun defend?

It would not take much to stir the Twilket and Aneza into another Nur-ed-Dam, despite the guests' peaceful departure the day after her and Faisal's handfasting.

Alaina's mouth twitched. Shahin of the Aneza had kissed her cheek, his beard tickling. Mey had hugged her, while Rashid smiled and shyly offered her a sand-lizard. Then with a deep bow, Zoltan gave her a beautifully carved wood inkwell, and wished her joy. Hala and Nimah had ridden away after tears and a kiss, declaring they would sail with her soon for Britannia. Basimah—well, she had given Alaina a handsome water bag for their journey into exile. Umar had disappeared sometime during the feast. And the wazir bestowed generous farewells on all.

Alaina shivered, and put her hand on Etain's warm neck. Everything came back to Sirius Abdasir. She scowled.

"My heart, what troubles you?"

She glanced at Faisal. "I wonder why we go to Britannia with the wazir. What does he seek there besides Kyrin?"

Her prince smoothed Truthseeker's breast feathers. The bird gently beaked his hand, and blinked farseeing eyes. "I do not think the wazir seeks gold," he said soberly. "There is far more across the south sea, with the black men. Trade, he may seek that. Your land has leather, silver, and artisans. Or he may seek men. Kyrin's father, Lord Dain Cieri, has many warriors, though if the wazir wishes men there are those far closer, like the Kathirib." Faisal looked at her. "There is also a tale from Baghdad of Hala's cousin. It is said her cousin Hamal disappeared in Britannia, that the wazir pays all who come to him with any word of his brother's son. There was an oath between them, I think."

Alaina pursed her mouth, noting the scents of hot horse, warm sand, and the sharp bitterness of desert herbs. Hala must have taken Hamal's name when she was captured. Then the wazir sent Kyrin, who found Hala. Had the wazir known it was Hala instead of Hamal from the beginning?

"My heart, I cannot come with you." Faisal frowned, staring between Zahir's ears. "Not to Britannia."

"What?" Alaina pulled Etain to an abrupt halt. "Why? Who says so? You must come!"

Faisal sighed. "Tae will not sail with the wazir. He wishes to reach Britannia before him." His nostrils flared. "Kentar brings word the Kathirib are gathering again. They buy swords, lances, horses, more men. Someone gave them gold. And Gershem—my grandfather could not rise at first, the morn we left. His legs sank under him." Faisal rubbed his face on his arm. "So Tae must go with you, and I must stay. I have Hafiz's blessing; we will fight the Kathirib together." Her prince smiled crookedly. "We will fall back to our mountains if the Kathirib do not find that another Alaina comes rushing down to overcome them. Also, the wazir did not ask me to go to Britannia. We think it best not to insist and stir his suspicion."

Alaina gaped at him, numb.

He tilted his head with a pained, wolfish smile. "I send Cicero with you, to guard you in my stead. And Gwenich, for Kyrin, as you asked."

Words fled. Alaina swallowed, her hands shaking on Etain's rein. So he and Tae had also wondered.

Thoughtfully, Faisal said, "Tae is a better guard than I."

So they would not sail with the wazir. Hala would be disappointed. But Faisal could not stay behind. She needed her prince. He needed her. She could not leave him. Blind, Alaina turned her head away, biting her lip.

Then Faisal's arms were around her, and he drew her down from the saddle. Alaina leaned against him and sobbed. Cicero whined and circled them, Sahar following, with the pups in a yipping melee.

Her prince kissed her long, then drew back and traced her mouth, his touch tender. "Alaina, you know we are but messengers, casting up the sand of peace in this world." He shrugged. "If it is not received, let the sand fall. It is the Master of the Stars' earth, and his wind, and we are the people of his hand. A gentle hand, far stronger than Umar's."

Alaina nodded. She laced her fingers in his and sniffed wetly.

Cicero barked. They walked after him, leading the horses. Alaina wiped her eyes.

A gazelle bolted, seeming to form out of the sand. Nine salukis stretched out in chase, their excited paws spurning the earth, yearning. Faisal cast Truthseeker into the sky. The falcon circled up. And stooped. Wings folded, she sped after Cicero, who dodged before the gazelle's churning hooves.

Faisal watched. Alaina watched him. The Master of all *did* wield a stronger, gentler hand than Umar in the world. They were a part of it, she a scop and her prince a sheyk, in heart and hand. She had chosen. A scop's heart she had gained, as the Master Scop shaped her.

When she turned to look inside herself at the word spoken, the thing written, the deed performed, her heart told her it was well. She pleased the Master of the Stars. Alaina's eyes pricked. He gave her so much in the desert: a greater heart, a prince, and a future. Not to mention a horse and a saluki, and friends near and far. She would come back to Hala and the others.

Faisal held out Etain's rein. Alaina met her prince's dark gaze, the challenge in the quirk of his mouth. And with a shaky grin, she took the leather and leaped for her saddle.

Etain galloped beside Zahir, and Alaina's hair streamed out. She drew Faisal's falcon brooch, pinned to the shoulder of her cloak, closer to her heart. She felt danger ahead. But it was time to meet it. Time to find Kyrin, and heal her heart's last ache.

They flowed over the sandy rise, a prince and his wife pursuing swift salukis, dawn-red and moon-pale, their pups running around them. Running, all four feet off the ground. Trusting it would be there when they landed.

The hunters. And the hunted.

15

Story Chat

*One theme of the book is truth. How does Alaina seek truth? Faisal? The others in the story? Does the way they seek truth affect the outcome of their circumstances? Does it affect them personally? How? How does seeking truth affect you?

*Alaina struggles with jealousy of Kyrin. Have you ever been jealous of someone? How did that end for you both? If you are still jealous, do you want to change that? Why?

*Truthseeker is a symbol in this book. What did you notice she represents, foreshadows, or affects?

*Kyrin writes to Alaina, "All men change, for evil or good—though often we cannot see it—above all, change in ourselves. Change is slow: thought on act, act on thought.

*In the beginning, Alaina seeks safety and despairs of recognition. How does that change by the end? Have you ever sought something, something that changed? What is something good that you seek now?

*At one point, Faisal knocks Alaina over in a sparring match. What does this mean to him? To her? Why is it important they acknowledge their different strengths?

*Another theme is love. What it is. What it isn't. Do you think Faisal and Alaina's growing knowledge of love is good?

Is it true? Why do you think so? Do you believe love is not true? Why?

*Cicero is a companion and protector to Alaina, far more than a pet. Have you ever had a dog like Cicero? How did they protect you? Comfort you?

*Betrayal. Who seems to betray Alaina and her prince, and who are the real betrayers? Have you ever been betrayed? Have you thought someone betrayed you and they didn't?

*What truths does Tae hunt, that tie into the next book? What does he suspect?

16

More Books

A reader of epic fantasy and new worlds, Azalea Dabill loves grand adventure and a satisfying, happy ending. Noblebright characters, the fate of the world, and tension between characters fascinates her. She will never stop learning about how words shape and hold meaning. Words wield power like a well-aimed bow.

Her debut novel was released in 2015. When she isn't writing you can find her growing things, raiding bookstores, or hiking the wild.

If you want to know more about her literary adventures you can join her here https://azaleadabill.com/ Her website is the hub for all her books, news, and reader resources. Kyrin's medieval adventures continue in Falcon Flight, and you can get your signed books from the author's website store and support her directly at https://azaleadabill.com/store/

It's usually cheaper than Amazon with shipping.

She is active on her Facebook page Mythic Fantasy https://www.facebook.com/azaleadabillmythicfantasy, or you can join her on Instagram https://www.instagram.com/azaleadabillauthor/?hl=en and GoodReads https://www.goodreads.com/author/show/13802917.Azalea_Dabill

Share Falcon Heart with a friend, Falcon Heart Wide Universal Book Link: https://books2read.com/u/bP1rpl. It's free!

Or tell me what could be improved or what you liked. Please leave a review on Amazon https://www.amazon.com/review/create-review/?ie=UTF8&channel=glance-detail&asin=B00VOEQXIO or at your favorite retailer. Thank you!

17

Sneak Peek: *Falcon Flight*

1

~Ruse~

... A PRINCE'S RUIN. ~PROVERBS 14:28

Kyrin Cieri strode toward the curtains of the Blue Flower room. More than two years of slavery. No word of home, her Britannia of rushing streams and whispering oaks, or of her father, Lord Dain Cieri of Cierheld.

And no way of escape.

Tae said the circle of circumstance was incomplete. Alaina told her the next stitch in the Master of the stars's pattern was not clear. Ali Ben Aidon guarded his slaves too well.

Would she ever walk in Cierheld with her father again? It was five years since her twelfth name-day, when she took the oath of first daughter in Cierheld hall. Esther would say she never had a first daughter's qualities, one who bore the old blood in her veins, and maybe she had not. Yet no one from home could call her "sprite get" now. She was stronger than they dreamed, though she carried the blood of the hills in her slight bones, dark hair and eyes.

She could not return to her people and her land. Her stronghold key rusted away in Ali's possession. She would not see her father again, and Cierheld would die with him.

Stronghold first daughter. She had never entirely felt like one. Kyrin bit her lip. Two things of Britannia remained to her.

Alaina Ilen, dearer than blood, her sister of salt and sacrifice, forged under threat of death. Walking at her side, Alaina's red-gold braid swung with a soft swish against her leather and cane body armor, laced over her white *thawb*. The intricately embroidered tunic displayed swords and flowers in delicate silver, blue and green. The staff Alaina held across her body was a harsh line dividing blade and bloom.

Kyrin's lips quirked. But for its leather handgrips, the staff was smooth as silk from Alaina's use. Her sister gave her a smart blow during their last training bout, before she wrested the weapon away. What new trick would Alaina bring against her this night, besides her proven mastery of the scribe's pen and her embroidery needle?

Ali's first bodyguard, watchful as a leopard, paced before heavy curtains of dark silk. With a glower, Umar thumped the hilt of his sword against the stone arch of the Blue Flower room. The solid thunk of his hilt announced their presence to the feasters within, and to their master, Ali Ben Aidon, merchant and murderer. Mouth wry, Kyrin dipped her head to Umar.

He held out his hand, demanding Alaina's staff. She laid the weapon in his palm, his skin nearer gold than white.

Kyrin wrinkled her nose. Her master's unacknowledged son could never quite wash off the smell of meat, rice, and saluki: the scents of the kennels, and the savage beasts of his Hand. Umar ran with them often, teaching his hunters of men patience and endurance in the desert sands. He glanced at her, expressionless.

Had he forgiven her for her eye of evil intent he once swore tipped the glowing brazier on Ali's ship, that gave him the burn scar across his sword hand?

No matter. Umar never spoke of it since. She had grown strong. She'd stolen every moment she could from serving Ali's table the past two winters to learn the demanding ways of *Subak*.

Tae Chisun, her husband in name, a second father in fact, had taught her well his ancestral fighting art of the hands and feet. Also, under the tutelage of her master's second bodyguard, Jachin, she knew one end of a sword from the other.

Umar glared at Alaina, free of her blue veil and serving robe for this brief moment, as he examined her staff for hidden blades. Umar never sought to interfere with Kyrin's training with Jachin, knowing their master wished her and Alaina's skill to impress the *caliph* in Baghdad—and those the caliph favored. Such as the caliph's *wazir*. Kyrin clenched her hand at her side.

She and Alaina would demonstrate the fighting art of the East to Ali's guests at table—and Sirius Abdasir. Once guardsman to the caliph, now first wazir, Ali's most honored guest professed a liking for close-in combat. So it would be dagger work this night, among other things. Kyrin touched her blade.

The cool haft of the weapon in her sash did not have the balance of her bronze falcon, the second thing that remained to her of Britannia. She'd left her mother's falcon dagger in their quarters. Tae was right.

Ali Ben Aidon must never discover the Damascus steel under the bronzed surface. It was her last gift from her mother. Never was the weapon for common wear. The falcon drew interest to its piercing amber gaze and beautiful strength.

Umar's smile widened, unpleasant. He kept Alaina's staff. "Wait until the master calls you."

Alaina glanced at Kyrin, who frowned. When would he let them in? He loved to play the sand cat with the mouse, she knew. But they were not his prey.

18

Fantastic Journey

Imaginative fiction is a key to our future. Beauty, mystery, and adventure are vital to our spirits. Fantastic journeys invite us to search beyond what we see for truth, to dig deeper for courage.

The soul of fantasy adventure benefits us on three levels:

~ The spiritual arena

~ The wide world of ideas

~ And the sphere we breathe in

Why do the quest and the hero's journey draw us all? What difference does it make? Have you ever wondered how to find the best fantasy adventures for your children, or your friends?

We bring up select jewels from the deep and explore mountain troves of fiction with seventy authors to whet your appetite for the riches heaped on untold shores. The inspiring adventures we explore are beacons of extraordinary story.

Most of them are lights by contrast, guiding us to enchanting lands of danger in the ocean of fantasy and speculative fiction. Heroes and heroines show us how to identify true gems and sell them not. How to discern enemies, friends, and endless possibilities with our inner eye, and to touch and to taste the truths of life in realms near and far. And we will discover that which is the wealth of souls.

Quote

Discover the Irresistible Beauty of Truth in Fantasy

Who does not wish that at least one moment in a beautiful epic fantasy were true? But some of those moments are true, and some of those places. The mystery of beauty, and sacrifice, the brave call of loyalty, and the torch of true relationships make us yearn for something we often cannot name. But we feel it in epic fantasies of courage, perseverance, and friendship that illuminate selflessness. We behold spiritual heights, physical depths, and in far realms we learn to refuse evil and choose good until it influences our adventures in our own sphere. Fantasy relates to deep reality.

Some people may say there is little truth in the ocean of fantasy. They claim the very words fantasy fiction are a double negative of reality. Others say that fantasy involves Wicca, witchcraft, magick—at the very least, it means New Age muddled thought. They claim fantasy is not for serious Christians because it does not encourage spirituality and faith. They say idealism or fantasy doesn't apply to real life, and abstract ideas in fantasy rarely touch real things.

In truth, real things and the ideals we hold are as closely connected as our body and spirit. Abstract ideals are intertwined in the physical and spiritual in every occurrence in the spatial universe. Every idea we believe, experience, and come to understand moves the breath, blood, and bone we call our body—because ideals first move our heart and spirit.

Fantasy mirrors reality, showing the abstract in sharper facets. It casts reality back at us in a thousand reflections, penetrating deeper into our souls at times than any physical blade on this earth.

19

Glossary

✳ These terms and names span the world of the Chronicle. Not every entry or book will have every word. Mispronunciations and mistakes are my own. For easier pronunciation I have reduced some words to phonetic spelling. May contain slight spoilers. Enjoy the adventure!

Britannia:

Armsman—"Arms-mun" a lord's sworn man who protects the lord's person and stronghold

Bells—Lauds "Lawds" (just before dawn), Prime (just after daybreak), Terce "Terse" (third hour), Sext (sixth hour), Nones "Nons" (ninth hour), Vespers (eleventh hour), Matins (just after midnight)

Britannia—"Bri-tan-ee-uh" ancient name for Britain

Brooch—"Broach" a pin often worn in pairs, used for cloaks

Death touch—Possible with a strong man trained in Subak—a death thought to be brought by a single blow. More often the culmination of several deadly nerve points or blows

Eagles—"E-gulls" an ancient name for Romans

Evil eye—Ali believes Kyrin can bring evil with her dark stare and brands her with a jet earring in her ear, besides his bronze ring of ownership in her other ear

Eyas—"Ee-ass" a young falcon in the nest

Eyrie—"Ear-ee" a falcon's nest high on a cliff

Falcon, Peregrine—"Pear-uh-grin" the bird Kyrin loves, which draws her to follow the Master of the stars

Falcon dagger—a mysterious dagger shaped like a falcon that Kyrin finds hidden in a cloak on her murdered mother's breast

Girdle—"Gir-dul" a kind of belt for women, often braided of leather or linen

Hose—like leggings but for men, usually fastened by cross garters to leather shoes

Mantle—"Man-tul" a woman's wrap, with a central hole for the head, like a poncho

Scop—"Shop" ancient name for a scribe, minstrel, bard

Stronghold key—a large key that signifies authority over a stronghold. Women often wore them on their girdles

Sigil—"sig-ill" a sign or mark on a letter, garment, or pennon, often indicating a house name or rank

Tunic—"Tune-ick" medieval shirt-like or robe-like garment for men and women, worn over an under-garment or shirt, often of linen, flowing to the knee for men and the feet for women

Names of important characters:

Aart—"A-art" Kyrin's horse, means like an eagle

Alaina Ilen—"A-lay-nuh I-len" Kyrin's peasant sister, closer than blood, means one who harmonizes, noble, stone

Aunt Medaen—"Ma-day-en" her father's tart-tongued sister who Kyrin hears in her head more than she'd like

Father Annis—"Ann-iss" an important monk who opposes Kyrin

Brother Rolf—"Rawl-f" a sympathetic monk who plays a part in Cierheld's fate

Father Ulf—Kyrin's uncle, pivotal to events in Falcon Flight

Berd—a young armsman in training who becomes Kyrin's armsman

Celine Loring—"Suh-lean Lore-ing" a childhood friend who antagonizes Kyrin. I liked the name for a red-haired girl

Etain—"E-tain" Alaina's mare in Araby, means fairy

Esther—a stronghold daughter, and Kyrin's beautiful rival

Cernalt—"Sir-nalt" an old armsman and hawkmaster to Lord Dain Cieri

Dain Cieri—"Dane Si-eery" Kyrin's father. His name fit the time and place, to my mind

Willa—"Will-a" Kyrin's mother. The connotations of the name fit her gentle strength

Elinore—Kyrin's step-mother, in honor of Sam's Elinore in LOTR. It sounded right

Gwenith—"Gwen-ith" the saluki pup that Alaina gives Kyrin, means blessed

Hal Loring—Celine's father and Kyrin's first student in Britannia

Kyrin Cieri—"Kai-rin Si-eery" I liked the sound, the name reminds me of dark hills, Celtic times, and Elizabeth Moon's Paksenarrion

Lord Bergrin Jorn—"Bur-grin Jorn" Myrna's brother, who holds Kyrin captive for a time, and is an ally in war

Lord Ludwin Mornoth—"Lud-win More-noth" Cierheld and the strongholds' nemesis

Lord Nidfael Keffer—"Nid-fi-el Keff-er" Mornoth's second in command, and Kyrin's nemesis

Meric—"Mare-ick" Kyrin's step-brother. His name fits his scholarly bent and nature

Myrna Jorn—"Mur-nuh" Kyrin's friend, means tender

Nell Trinley—a girl with mismatched eyes that Kyrin rescues, who becomes a healer

Nith—an armsmaster, first in command of Cierheld in *Falcon Flight*

Ragad—"Ra-gad" shipmaster of the Howler, Sirius Abdasir's ship that brings Kyrin on her task to find Hamal

Seliam—"See-li-am" the wazir's slave, an askar who threatens everyone Kyrin loves in *Falcon Heart*

Sirius Abdasir—"Sear-ee-us Ab-da-sir" wazir to the caliph, who holds the secret of the falcon dagger and threatens to destroy Kyrin and all of Cierheld

Talik—"Tal-ick" a messenger between the strongholds who rescues Kyrin, who loves and quarrels with her

The Master of the stars—the meaning of this name is for you to discover

Wolf-ship warrior—another name for a Viking

White Christer—a Viking's name for one who follows Christ

§

Araby/Arabia:

Aba—"Ab-uh" an Arabian women's cloak

Aneza—"A-nez-uh" a tribe of Araby people in Kyrin's world

Askar—"Ass-car" means fighter, warrior

Bisht—"Bish-it" Araby men's cloak

Bedu/Bedouin—"Bed-du" or "Bed-o-in" a name for those who live in the desert

Caliph—"Kal-iph" Araby ruler in Baghdad

Dalil—"Dal-lil" a caravan guide, often across the desert

Djinn—"Jin" jinn, genie, jinni

Empy Quarter—Al Ramlah, the ocean of sand south and inland of the coastal mountains

Hattah—"Hat-tah" desert women's light head covering. Not a veil, though it can be used to cover the face

Kaffiyeh—"Ca-fi-yuh" Araby men's head covering

Mahr—"Marr" a desert maiden's dowry, often precious metal anklets, bracelets, and coins sewn into a bridal headpiece or veil

Nargeela—"Nar-gee-la" a water pipe

Nasrany—"Nas-rany" an infidel unbeliever

Nur-ed-Dam—"Nur-ed-dom" the oath of the Light of Blood, or blood-feud oath

Reem—the black-horned gazelle and others of its kind

Shaheen—"Sha-heen" Arabic for a falcon, also the name given to Kyrin

Sheyk—"Shay-ick" a desert leader of a tribe, such as Gershem Ben Salin of the Twilkets

Souk—"Sook" an Araby market

Thawb—"Thaw-ub" an Araby tunic

Twilkets—"Twil-kets" an enemy tribe until events bring unforeseen secrets to light

Umar's Hand—"Oo-mar's Hand" Umar's pack of salukis he trained against their gentle nature to hunt men

Wadi—"Wad-ee" a watercourse, usually dry except during the rainy season

Wazir—"Wah-zeer" the advisor to the caliph

Names of important characters:

Ali Ben Aidon—"Ali-ben A-don" Araby slaver, a common Arabic name

Basimah—"Bass-i-mah" means one who smiles

Cicero—"Siss-er-o" Kyrin and Alaina's saluki, named after a wise man

Faisal—"Fie-sel" desert prince of the Twilkets, loves both Kyrin and Alaina. Means a wise, just judge

Farook—"Fa-ruke" the wazir's slave forced to betray Alaina, means one who discerns right and wrong

Gershem Ben Salin—"Ger-shem Ben Sa-lin" Twilket sheyk and Faisal's grandfather. I liked the name

Hafiz—"Ha-feez" first warrior, and Alaina's opponent in *Lance and Quill*. Means the guardian

Hala—"Hall-uh" Sirius Abdasir's daughter, means halo around the moon

Hamal—"Ha-mall" the wazir's lost traveler, means gentle as a lamb

Jachin—"Ja-chin" Ali's bodyguard and Tae's friend. I liked the sound for a friendly Nubian

Kentar—"Ken-tar" a caravan guide and Tae's eyes and ears. I liked the name from *The Blue Sword*

Mey—"May" Shahin's wife and Rashid's mother. I liked the sound of the name

Nara—"Nar-uh"Umar's Egyptian mother, Ali's cook, and Kyrin's friend in Ali's house, meaning unknown

Nimah—"Nim-uh" first to welcome Kyrin and Alaina to Ali's house, means blessing

Neddra—"Ned-druh" an Aneza girl who admired Kyrin's falcon dagger, the sound drew me

Qadira—"Ka-deer-uh" head concubine in Ali's house, means powerful one

Rashid—"Ra-shid" the young sheyk's son, means the well guided

Sahar—"Saw-har" Faisal's red saluki, means the dawn

Sarni—"Sar-nee" the name a desert prince gives Alaina, means the elevated one

Shahin—"Sha-hin" sheyk of the Aneza, shelters Kyrin during the desert war for saving his son, Rashid

Truthseeker—the falcon eyas the Aneza tribe gives Kyrin

Umar—"Oo-mar" Ali's treacherous and unacknowledged son, means flourishing, long-lived

Zahir—"Za-heer" Faisal's stallion, means shining, radiant

Zoltan—"Zol-tan" Nimah's brother, means a ruler

§

Land of the Morning Calm/Korea:

Ap bal Chagi—"Op-ball-chagi" front-kick—a snapping kick that best attacks the groin or stomach

Barow—"Ba-row" means return to starting position

Chin-gol—"Chin-goal" means true bone. It was one of the highest military ranks after head-rank five.

Choson—"Cho-san" a name for the early Korean culture, specifically applied in my books to the Silla dynasty

Death touch—Possible with a strong man trained in Subak. A death thought to be brought by a single blow, but more often the culmination of several deadly nerve points or blows

Dojang—"Doh-jong" a place of learning for Subak

Dwi Chagi—"Dwee-chagi" a back-kick. The strongest kick, this one stops an attacker like a stone wall

Hwarang—"Huh-waa-rang" flowering warrior or leader of 500 to 5,000 hwarangdo—one trained in martial arts, literature, the arts, sciences, and one hundred and eight different weapons

Jun be—"June-bee" stance ready for attack. There are several variations

Kum-sool—"Come-sool" means sword skill

Kuksun—"Kook-sun" a commander or general, a lord who led by example

Naryu Chagi—"Nari-yu-chagi" an axe-kick or spinning kick often used to attack enemies on horseback

Open hand—attack with the fingers, palm, or knife-edge of the hand to the eyes, temples, neck, etc.

Pil Sung—certain victory through courage, strength, and indomitable spirit

Poomse—"Poom-say" a sequence of training techniques done in flowing order, often with multiple techniques hidden within

Hwarangdo—"Huh-waw-rang-doh" or "Rang-do" a martial art student who learned under a hwarang master and followed Sesokokye

Seajok—"Say-jock" a command to begin (the fight, etc.)

Seon—"Say-on" Tae-shin or Tae Chisun, after his name was changed—left Seon to follow the Master of the stars, means the way of Zen

Sesokokye—"See-sok-o-kye" be loyal to your country, honor your parents, be faithful to your friends, never retreat in battle, use good judgment before killing any living thing.

Silla—A dynasty spanning the first century B.C. to 935 A.D. Our story happens around 830 or 840 A.D.

Subak—"Soo-bok" a component of Tae-shin's way of the warrior, means hand technique

Tiger—a beast of terrible power that haunts Kyrin's dreams

Yeop Chagi—"Yee-op chagi" side-kick. This can cripple, used against the knee at an angle

Names of important characters:

Cho Seung—"Cho-sung" Tae-shin's treacherous Hwarang master, means candle, beginning, or second, and rise or acheive

Jeong Jin-ho—"Jee-ong Jin-ho" the rebel kuksun who honors Tae-shin when he is cast outside his clan as a traitor. Means quiet or loyal, and great, brave, heroic, or chivalrous

Ha-nuel—"Ha-new-ul" Tae-shin's brave student who carried an essential message for the life of his people, means sky

Ryung-suk—"Ree-ung Sook" Tae's son born while he is in exile, means bright rock

Kim Jin-dae—"Jin-day" the name of Tae-shin/Tae Chisun's wife, means truth, or jewel, and greatness. "Huen" (pet name) may be associated with judgement. "Kim" means gold.

Kim Paekche—"Pack-chi" is Tae-shin's father-in-law who exiled him. "Kim" means gold, "Paekche" is thought to mean one hundred crossings.

Ryu Tae-shin—"Rue Tie-shin" where "Ryu" means willow tree, "Tae-shin" means great, and belief, faith, or trust. He came to be named Tae Chisun "Tie Chee-sun" by his captor, in his exile. Tae (great) is the first name of a grandmaster, Tae Hong Choi. I also liked the sound for a hero's name. "Choi," as in Master Choi in *Path of the Warrior*, means governor of the land and the mountain, or high, superior, lofty.

Young-sool—means dragon or valiant one, and martial art technique

20

Acknowledgements

There are too many wonderful people who assisted me on my writing journey to name them all. So, if your name is not here and you dropped a word of encouragement or helped me on my writing journey, know that I appreciate you very much.

My thanks to my dad, mom, and family for their support in so many ways, and to Sandy Cathcart, Lynn Leissler, Jeanette Windle, Susan May Warren, and Kathi Macias for their teaching and encouragement at pivotal points in my writing.

And I could never get far without my crit group, Fantasy for Christ. My deepest thanks to you.

More recently during the book updates, I thank Charlotte Lesemann and Emily Moore for their encouragement, beta reading, and help with the things that make a book worthwhile.

And I also thank you, my readers. You're the best! I deeply appreciate your invaluable advice and honest reviews!

If you have not reviewed this book yet, you can leave a review on Amazon https://www.amazon.com/review/

create-review/?ie=UTF8&channel=glance-detail&asin=B00VOEQXIO or at your favorite retailer if you want to let the world know how you liked it. As the author, I highly value your feedback and insights, as does the rest of the reading world. Thank you!

Azalea Dabill ~ Crossover – Find the Eternal, the Adventure